"Temple of Diamonds"

My Return to Judaism and Other Essays

CHAIM PICKER

iUniverse, Inc.

New York   Bloomington

iUniverse books may be ordered through booksellers or by contacting:

iUniverse
1663 Liberty Drive
Bloomington, IN 47403
www.iuniverse.com
1-800-Authors (1-800-288-4677)

Because of the dynamic nature of the Internet, any Web addresses or
links contained in this book may have changed since publication and may
no longer be valid. The views expressed in this work are solely those of
the author and do not necessarily reflect the views of the publisher, and
the publisher hereby disclaims any responsibility for them.

ISBN: 978-1-4401-6046-2 (sc)
ISBN: 978-1-4401-6047-9 (ebook)

Printed in the United States of America

iUniverse rev. date:10/08/2009

Preface

"Temple of Diamonds"

A word of explanation for the title, "Temple of Diamonds": Later in my book, the reader will encounter an essay with this title, inspired by a winter-walk to Temple on a Shabbat in the aftermath of a severe winter-ice-storm. The trees were clad in ice which, loosened by the warming sun, were cascading downward, littering the ground with sparkling "diamonds" which yielded a riotous spectrum of color. It was a journey through a "Temple of Diamonds."

As I mused about a possible title for my book, my thoughts were drawn back to this experience and another meaning for "Temple of Diamonds" occurred to me: When, many years prior, upon my return to Judaism after a fifteen-year sojourn in a "strange land," my initial destination was Temple Israel. Considering my resume, I easily and justifiably expected a questionable reception. But I was welcomed with brotherly love and understanding by the Temple Israel congregational family. There must have been misgivings, I thought, about the young man who, at the age of fifteen, had opted for Christianity. On the contrary, however, I was warmly embraced, asked to speak about my experience and, remarkably, invited to teach the children of Temple Israel. My benefactor was Shraga Arian, who had faith in me and recognized my potential as a teacher. Subsequently, I was entrusted with the Shabbat-morning junior congregation and later with the inestimable privilege of serving as the congregation's surrogate in prayer-the Hazzan!

Diamonds, precious and rare, when skillfully faceted, catch the light and refract its prismatic colors. Temple Israel has "caught" and "faceted" me, enabling me to utilize my teaching and musical gifts. The opportunities afforded me in Temple Israel have been precious beyond price. "Diamonds"!

A temple may serve as a sanctuary, a refuge, a site for contemplation, comfort and inspiration. All these have accrued to me in Temple Israel. In Temple Israel, I and my family have acquired precious friends who have enriched our lives. More treasured "diamonds."

Last and most beloved, I remember my cherished soulmate Martha, my diamond, who, like the biblical Ruth, came with me to Judaism – along with our three children Donald, Joyce and Joel – to take shelter under the wings of the Holy One of Israel. She too was warmly welcomed by the Temple Israel family and Jewish community, serving as secretary of Temple Israel, the Bet Shraga Hebrew Academy and president of Albany Bat Ami Hadassah. Martha was beloved and respected as an *Eshet Chayil* – a woman of valor. *Zichronah Livrachah* – her memory is for a blessing!

What I have written here would not and could not have been written had our family not found our "Temple of Diamonds" - Temple Israel. With gratitude, therefore, I dedicate this book to the Temple Israel Congregational Family.

Chaim Picker, Albany, N.Y.
24 Tamuz, 5769 – 24 June, 2009
cpic18@verizon.net
518-438-3084 (Land)
518-265-1382 (Mobile)

Acknowledgements:

I am indebted to my faithful and cherished friend Dr. Sandor Schuman, who gave unstintingly of his time and consummate computer skills to format my manuscript and to my friend Bob Neudel for his masterful cover photos. These individuals are among the diamonds I have discovered and treasured in the Temple Israel congregational family.

Contents

Introduction

This is not an autobiography in the usual sense. It is an account of a spiritual journey; a portrait of what has defined my life as a Jew. It is about human values as seen through one man's eyes; for Judaism, at essence, is the embodiment of universal human values.

My son recently said to me, "Dad, you're all about religion and attending synagogue." Unfortunately, my son saw only the outward appearance of what transpires in his dad's life. As often occurs between parents and children, emotions block the pathways of spiritual communication. Where verbal communication may fail, however, the written word may succeed. It is my hope, therefore, my children will take this book in hand and discover their dad's deepest longings, philosophy of life and values as a Jew and human being. That it will provide guidance and inspiration, lighten their burden, ease their path through life and help them understand that Judaism is more than ritual observance and that its guiding principle is to teach us how to be wholly human.

What I have written has been told myriads of times. But I must tell it again—for my children, for my friends and for my students. Indeed, each one is privileged to retell the story of life as he sees and experiences it, for there is something of value to learn from everyone: "Who is wise He who learns from everyone" (Pirke Avot 4:1). Scripture says, "Of the making of books there is no end" (Ecclesiastes 12:12). Notwithstanding, every individual has a unique story and no spiritual journey is superfluous.

This book is not intended as an exhaustive survey of Jewish values but a glimpse into ideas I personally have cherished and that have defined my life. We start life as a seed, full of potential growth. As we grow, we gather knowledge, understanding and experience. Hopefully, our tree of life bears the fruits of character and good deeds.

Having reached and surpassed the age of eighty – the "age of strength" (Pirke Avot 5:25) – I could justifiably sit back, pamper myself and obsess on physical infirmities. For many, unfortunately, eighty is not the age of *physical* strength. It may, however, be a time of *spiritual* strength, when one is accorded respect and honor and sought after for guidance. Said the preacher, "In the morning sow your seed and in the evening withhold not your seed" (Ecclesiastes 11:6). The Midrash comments: "If you have had children in your youth, take a wife in old age and beget children" (Genesis Rabah 61:3). I append my own midrashic interpretation: If you have taught children in your youth, continue teaching in your old age (cf. Psalms 92:15).

Some achieve fame and fortune and endow hospitals, universities, schools and museums, which are named after them. Only a few are privileged to attain this. But virtually everyone has a story to tell that will enrich the pool of human wisdom and experience. We write wills, bequeathing material possessions to our heirs. Judaism has a tradition of "ethical wills." This book is in the manner of an ethical will. In Judaism we refer to our departed loved ones with, "May his/her memory be for a blessing." The memory and example of our deceased loved ones surely may be an example to help define our lives. But memory is fragile, fading like the morning mist. What remains for future generations may be only an epitaph on a memorial stone. My father was a vastly creative man, gifted inventor and musician. Sadly, however, I do not possess a single written word from him — only photos and a mandolin he created out of a tennis racket which hangs on the wall of my study. How I would have cherished words of wisdom from him! How I long to know what was in his heart and his inner struggles! It is a melancholy thought to contemplate the many human beings whose lives were exemplary – who had exceptional wisdom but went to their graves unsung and unrecorded.

I am neither sage nor person of fame; but I must do what lies within me. Scripture admonishes, "Do with your might what your hands find to do" (Ecclesiastes 9:10). It is *your* hands, not another's. Your hands may not always find great things to do but you must do what *you* are uniquely capable of doing. The Mishneh teaches: "A human being mints coins with one stamp and all are alike. God stamps everyone with the stamp of Adam and all are different. Therefore one should say: 'The world was created for my sake'" (Sanhedrin, ch. 4, Mishneh III). Every human being sees and experiences the world in a unique way. The Mishneh again teaches: "It is not yours to complete the work but neither are you free to desist from it" (Pirke Avot 2:21). We may not be the best to perform a given task but we are nonetheless obligated to attempt it.

When God sent Moses to Pharaoh to demand the release of the Hebrew slaves, Moses demurred, saying: "Who am I that I should go before Pharaoh ...?" (Exodus 3:11). We must never think of ourselves as insignificant. Our sages remind us that if we are feeling unworthy, we should remember we were created in the image of God (Genesis 1:26, 27; 5:1).

Honi the Circle-maker, a first-century sage, was walking along a road when he saw a man planting a Carob tree. "How long will it take this tree to bear fruit?" asked Honi. "Seventy years," replied the man. "And are you certain you will live seventy years to enjoy its fruits?" continued Honi. Replied the man, "I found the world with Carob trees. As my fathers planted for me, so I plant for my children" (Baba Bathra 23). As the beneficiary of the rich fruits of wisdom of our sages,

I am duty-bound to continue their heritage. As my teachers planted for me, I plant for those who shall come after me.

1

Conversion to Christianity and
Return to Judaism

To change one's ancestral religion is a basic human right. Abraham abandoned the idolatrous religion of his father. Abraham's Jewish descendants sometimes see fit to abandon their ancestral heritage. When Jews change their religion, invariably they become passionate devotees of their new-found faith, rarely finding their way back to Judaism. Those who do return are scrutinized, even more so than new converts, because of lingering doubts about their sincerity.

Jews who convert to other religions usually have only a superficial knowledge of their ancestral heritage; but, characteristically, they approach their new religion with zeal and diligence. Whereas they may have been indifferent regarding their birth-religion, there is a sense of adventure and challenge regarding the newly adopted religion: "Stolen waters are sweet and bread eaten in secret is pleasant" (Proverbs 9:17). Though the Jewish convert may reinvestigate Judaism after conversion, his studies invariably are colored by his newly acquired doctrines and are pursued to enhance his missionary proficiency – often aimed at enlisting other Jews.

MY ROOTS

My father, Charles (Kusiel) Picker, was born in 1896, in Horodyszcze, White Russia – one of five children of Yehudah-Leb and Haya-Rachel Pochapovsky. Tradition has it that

1

an ancestor came from Pochapovo, a village about fifteen kilometers distant. When Grandfather Lebe came to the United States, he changed his name to Picker. Grandfather was a tall, handsome man, with a small beard who, as a young man, had studied cantorial music in Odessa with the famed Cantor Resumne.

As a boy of eleven, my father fashioned his own violin and climbed an Alder tree in the forest where he played his instrument. In 1913, at the age of seventeen, he came to the United States, settling in Albany, New York. In 1918, combining his musical and mechanical talents, he created a number of original musical instruments, featuring his "musical bottles," or "musical organ," which he performed at the Grand Theater in Albany and in New York City. Though my father was not religious, he was a proud Jew. My paternal grandparents died before I was born.

My mother, Yetta Goldstein, was born in 1906, in Brooklyn, New York. She married my father Charles in Albany, in 1925. My maternal grandfather Arye Leb ("Zaida") prayed every morning with *tefillin* (phylacteries). His Passover Seder, attended by all the uncles and aunts, was the family event of the year. As the youngest child, I was expected to ask the "four questions," both in Yiddish and Hebrew. Grandmother Rachel ("Bubi") was a gentle, pious soul. As the first grandchild and only grandson, I was favored. On the Sabbath, my bubi would light five candles in her silver candlestick. She had a "pushke" (charity box), into which she would deposit pennies. I remember her once asking me to take some pennies down to an itinerant. My bubi didn't moralize, but her example of *tsedakah* (charity), simple piety and goodness, shines brightly in my memory.

At the age of eight, I attended a *heder* (one-room Hebrew school), at 140 Grand Street, in Albany, New York. Our teacher, Mr. Aurbach, an immigrant from Europe, was a stern but skillful instructor who taught us Hebrew and Yiddish.

Bible study was a dry exercise of translating and fact-culling, with philosophical questions brushed aside. Sabbath services were held weekly, joyfully attended by the students. The hymn *Adon Olam* was a favorite because it was followed by a *Kiddush* of honey cake and wine. As a youngster I had questions and yearned for a sympathetic listener – someone who would take me seriously. That person proved to be my mother's youngest brother – Uncle Joe . . . .

UNCLE JOE

In the 1930's, Uncle Joe, a gifted artist, was seeking employment when he met Arthur, son of a prominent Jewish manufacturing family. Arthur, a creator of children's games for The American Toy Company, hired Joe as a game-illustrator. Arthur was a Jehovah's Witness who claimed to have had a "vision" of Jesus and was converted. Under his tutelage and charismatic personality, Joe became a Jehovah's Witness.

Uncle Joe had grown up in an orthodox home, attending synagogue with his father. Possessed of an artistic temperament, he was restless, inquisitive and given to experimentation. He regarded Judaism as perfunctory. Jehovah's Witnesses, however, led by the charismatic and fiery Judge Rutherford, with its sensational message of the world's imminent end and coming New World, fervent door-to-door preaching and spectacular conventions – these ignited Uncle Joe's imagination. He once expressed his abhorrence of ticket-selling in the synagogue on the High Holidays and his dissatisfaction with prayers said in an unintelligible language. His Judaism at best was superficial.

PASSOVER SEDER, 1938

In 1938, at the age of twelve, I had been visiting my maternal grandparents in Brooklyn during Passover. At the Passover Seder, Uncle Joe remained in his room, doing art work.

A bitter argument ensued between him and his brothers. Because of my love for my uncle, my sympathies were with him. It was then I first learned of his new religion –initiating a dialogue that would change my life . . . .

THE KINGDOM HALL

As my uncle began "witnessing" to me, the idea of a "new world" captured my imagination. On one of my visits to Brooklyn, he took me to the "Kingdom Hall," located on a third floor in a commercial building in the Flatbush area. On the large windows that faced the street, lettered in gold, were the words, "Kingdom Hall of Jehovah's Witnesses." Nervously following my uncle up two flights of stairs, I entered a brightly lit, spotless hall and was introduced to the "brothers and sisters." I was impressed with these young, clean-cut staff people from the Watchtower headquarters in Brooklyn. Sitting next to my uncle listening to a speaker, I was startled when I heard the name "Jesus Christ" mentioned. Since this name had never come up in our discussions, I had no inkling my uncle's new religion was Christian. Alarmed and puzzled, I turned to my uncle and was assured he would explain. Later in his car, he took out a limp, black leather Bible from the glove-compartment and began to show me prophecies from the Old Testament.

MY PARENTS' ANGUISH

Upon learning of my interest in Jehovah's Witnesses, my parents reacted vehemently. Uncle Joe was not deterred. He believed my "eternal life" took precedence over my parents' anguish. Citing the first commandment of obedience to God, he explained how it *preceded* the commandment to honor father and mother – thereby "conditioning" me for parental hostility and telling me I must be willing to "suffer for righteousness' sake."

I was preparing for my Bar Mitzvah to take place June

14, 1939, at Congregation Beth El Jacob on Herkimer Street. The Torah portion was Balak, containing the words, "How goodly are your tents, O Jacob, your tabernacles, O Israel." The *haftorah* (prophetic portion) was Micah, chapter 5, concluding with the words, "Will the Lord be pleased with thousands of rams, with ten thousands of rivers of oil? Shall I give my first-born for my transgressions . . . It has been told thee . . . what the Lord requires of thee but to do justly, love mercy and walk humbly with thy God." I didn't fully understand the significance of these words but in later years I would. As my Bar Mitzvah ceremony was ending, I approached the Torah ark, took hold of a corner of the curtain and recited, "May the words of my mouth and the mediation of my heart be acceptable before Thee, O Lord, my Rock and my Redeemer." Even at that youthful age, my soul was agitated as I meditated on another religion, wondering whether indeed it *was* acceptable to God.

LINGERING QUESTIONS

Despite my uncle's persuasiveness, I had lingering questions and was not ready to abandon my religion. Believing my Hebrew teacher was "all-knowing" and surely could refute my uncle, I asked him to confront my uncle at my Bar Mitzvah-reception. To my deep disappointment, he failed to do so. My parents applied pressure and my other uncles ridiculed my uncle Joe – which only drew me closer to him. I resented their use of emotional tactics rather than reason. By contrast, Uncle Joe was gentle, loving and fatherly, reinforcing my self-confidence and supplying me with a steady flow of Watchtower publications, which I avidly studied, sending off questions to him. Fearing my parents constantly were watching me, I would I hide my letters and literature. My uncle and I developed a ruse. He would write to the family, using the words "general," or "generally" — code-words signaling mail awaited me at the "General Delivery" window at the main post office – which I would claim under the assumed name "Howard Harvey." Perceiving my parents as adversaries to be outwitted, this bit of "high drama" titillated me.

FATHER'S FATAL ILLNESS

In the spring of 1943, my father was stricken with a fatal heart-ailment. His illness was a period of deep, soul-searching for me. Part of me felt pity and filial love for this once fiercely, independent man, struck down so early by illness – whose pain I had compounded by my religious tactics. Another part of me yielded to the shameful temptation of imagining how wonderfully free I would be to pursue my religious activities. My father died on April 10, 1943, at the age of 47. I was sixteen. At his burial, I felt obliged as a "faithful witness of Jehovah," to express words of hope for the dead. My act typified the zeal of Jehovah's Witness who believe it is their sacred obligation to "bear witness" at every opportunity.

My witness-activities intensified. I obtained the address of the local Kingdom Hall, at 448 Broadway in downtown Albany. After the modern Kingdom Hall in Brooklyn, this dingy, cramped place was a disappointment. But my religious zeal overcame my disappointment and I attended my first meeting. There were few young people present and I befriended an elderly, blind, black man – Brother Bill Jackson. I was pleasantly surprised to learn the leader of the Kingdom Hall, a short, balding man with a German accent, was a Jew. In those early days of uncertainty, the presence of a Jew in Jehovah's Witnesses was reassuring.

I began "witnessing" on Sunday mornings near my home in the Lincoln Park area. In those days the "door-step set up" was used. When a householder answered the door, we would play a four-minute phonograph-recording of Judge Rutherford and then present the literature. The message of the "New World of peace and plenty" appealed to the poor and disadvantaged. We carried a booklet with testimonies in thirty languages. When, for example, an Italian immigrant opened the door, I would read the testimony in Italian. On other occasions, I stood on major street corners, hawking the Watchtower. This anguished my mother, who was tormented by derisive comments from her friends. On one occasion, my cousin confronted me on the street corner and chastised me for leaving my mother alone in the store. Though I continued to run the family store, I neglected it because of my witness activities. I taught in the Kingdom Hall, gave public lectures and conducted home Bible studies. Many of the homes I visited were poor. A householder would sometimes interrupt a lesson to squash a cockroach. I learned to avoid upholstered chairs in favor of hard kitchen chairs. In my naiveté and youthful zeal, I was oblivious to danger as I witnessed in the slums of the inner city. Black people, hospitable and gracious, provided a fertile field for witnessing. One black mother with whom I studied would nurse her baby in my presence. Another served me her delicious, steaming, sweet potato pie. I converted a number of black people, one of whom subsequently became the leader of the local Kingdom Hall.

UNCLE MAURICE

Uncle Joe's older brother Maurice, a lawyer and banker, well versed in Judaism, tried continuously to dissuade me from my path. Attempting to undermine my faith in my uncle Joe, he would denigrate him, calling him gullible. In my youthful arrogance, I resented Uncle Maurice's insinuation that I was too young and inexperienced to make judgments regarding Judaism and Christianity. This touched a "raw nerve," hinting at a problem I had faced from the beginning – frustration at not being taken seriously.

DOUBTS

As a young man, I was so awed – some would say "brain-washed" – by the teachings of the Watchtower Society, that I could not conceive of anyone defecting. I naively asked my uncle one day if he knew of any defections. He knew of only a few. Whereas for most religious people, theology is not critical, for Jehovah's Witnesses it is crucial. With heavy emphasis on doctrine, they are a missionary society and require uncompromising acceptance of all their teachings. Catholics may entertain second thoughts about the virgin-birth and papal infallibility. Jews may question the biblical miracles. But Jehovah's Witnesses may not doubt.

Until the early 1950's, my faith had been unshakable. I was convinced every question had an answer, divinely revealed through "God's organization," the Watchtower Society. We were "in the Truth." But the inquiring spirit which drove my initial rebellion was still present. Just as that spirit had turned a critical searchlight on Judaism, now, in the early 1950's, it began to refocus on my beliefs as a Jehovah's Witness.

On a visit to my uncle in the summer of 1954, we were sitting at a lunch counter in Manhattan when I turned to my uncle and asked: "Have you ever found yourself doubting the truthfulness of the gospel-accounts of Jesus?" Taken aback, he replied: "Why do you ask?" I replied, "I have been re-reading the gospels lately and, frankly, I find them hard to believe!" My uncle, rarely at a loss for words, was stunned. A few days before, I had taken up my Bible and was examining a passage in the gospels. Becoming engrossed, I had continued reading the New Testament for several days. I had not read this way for some time. My reading invariably had been desultory, searching for source-material for talks. This time I was reading *purely*, without commentaries. It seemed like a new book to me. Gradually the feeling began to grow that it was all too incredible – that I could no longer give it my assent. I found myself questioning the very foundations of

my faith — my life's commitment! It was as if a curtain had
been lifted and a new light was illuminating my life. How
this could have happened after fifteen years of indoctrination,
I do know. If anyone had tried to refute my beliefs, it only
would have provoked a passionate defense. Any challenge had
to come from within. My doubting had happened gradually,
impalpably. I began to reinvestigate the pivotal Jehovah's
Witness doctrine of the "144,000," the supposed "heavenly"
class of Jehovah's Witnesses who are chosen to be priests and
kings in heaven, while the rest of the Jehovah's Witnesses are
destined for an earthly reward. This class had allegedly been
filled by the 1930's. The "remnant" still remaining on earth
constitutes God's messengers of truth and they alone partake
of the bread and wine at the yearly "memorial" service of Jesus'
last supper. I re-examined Revelation, chapter 7, the source
of this teaching, and concluded the Watchtower Society had
misinterpreted it. The 144,000 and the great multitude are
both before the throne of God. They are natural Israelites.
The "great multitude" constitutes the Gentile believers. I
had challenged a fundamental Watchtower teaching. Until
now, my faith had remained unshakable. Any doubts I might
have had were attributed to a lack of understanding. With
"more light" they would be clarified. Now convinced the
"infallible" Watchtower Society had erred in a major doctrine,
the floodgates of inquiry were opened. (The New Testament
vision of the 144,000 and the Watchtower interpretation seem
quite irrelevant to me today. At that time of my spiritual
struggle, however, it was a crucial issue.)

The meticulous doctrinal structure of Jehovah's Witnesses,
on the one hand, is a strength, insuring loyalty. On the other
hand, it is a weakness, for a "perfect" system is vulnerable. Like
a single puncture in a balloon, one imperfection threatens
the entire structure. The illusion of a divinely inspired
organization having been shattered, I now summoned the
courage to examine other Watchtower teachings. The

Watchtower teaches this is the "Day of Judgment;" that there is no salvation outside the organization. Non-believers, despite being good people, will perish at Armageddon. My grandparents, who were kind, loving and righteous people, had had ample opportunity to hear the Watchtower's teachings from their son, explained eloquently and patiently in their native Yiddish tongue. But they rejected its message. I recoiled at the thought of their perishing.

My uncle and Arthur made an urgent trip to visit me in East Greenbush. Sitting with me for hours, they tried to convince me of the error of my ways – but to no avail. Although I took exception to the Watchtower teachings, they assured me I need not disassociate – as long as I kept my beliefs private. The real crisis developed when my views became public.

BLOOD TRANSFUSION

The Watchtower of July 1, 1954, stated: "Blood transfusion, even to save a life, violates God's covenant." Although I had long doubted this teaching, I had obediently put my doubts aside. Now that I was no longer subject to the Watchtower Society, the irrationality of this teaching had become strikingly clear. I could no longer accept a doctrine that required the needless sacrifice of life and contradicted God's justice and mercy.

On October 19, 1955, I received a telephone call. The distraught caller related that her mother Katie, a Jehovah's Witness whom I had once mentored, was in the Albany Hospital. Having suffered severe internal bleeding, she was in urgent need of a blood-transfusion but would not consent to it. When I arrived at the hospital, I found the daughter highly agitated. Holding me responsible for her mother's plight, her first words were, "Well, does she or doesn't she get a transfusion?" I conferred with the doctor who confirmed that without a blood-transfusion the patient would not survive. Weakly, Katie asked me what to do. I replied, "Do you remember what the Watchtower once said, 'A live witness is better than a dead one.'"? (This may not have been wholly accurate but it didn't matter to me at the time.) She consented to a transfusion, a clip board with a waiver was brought and I guided her hand as she signed it. Katie recovered and remained a Jehovah's Witness. When the Jehovah's Witness officials learned of my intervention, I was disfellowshipped. Rather than a punishment, I considered it an honor. (Twelve years later, in 1967, having refused a blood transfusion, Katie died.) The blood-transfusion drama strengthened my resolve. I began to re-read the New Testament. When I finished, I realized I was no longer a Christian.

Already a year previous to the blood-transfusion incident, I had been thinking of my identity. My maternal grandmother had died on September 16, 1954, co-incident with the time I had begun questioning the Watchtower teachings. At her grave, I had put on a kippah. (This unnerved my uncle Joe.) Now, memories of her righteous and loving soul began to stir deep searchings.

RETURN

I was managing our gift and lamp shop on South Pearl Street in downtown Albany when a new custodian for the building was hired. We became friends. It turned out he and his wife were survivors of the Warsaw ghetto. Recounting the indescribable sufferings of the Jews, He related how he had returned home one day, only to learn his father, mother and young son had been murdered by the Nazis. He brought me a copy of Emmanuel Ringleblum's *Notes of the Warsaw Ghetto*. As I read it, my heart ached for my people, from whom I had distanced myself during the period of their greatest calamity. I wept for them, the tears burning away the scales from my eyes. As I began to feel my true Jewish identity, a deep longing welled up within me to return to my people. Seized with an insatiable desire to read every book on Judaism I could find, I visited the New York State Library and met the chief reference librarian—a Jewish lady. We became acquainted and she permitted me to go into the stacks where I eagerly perused the collection of Judaica. Like a child in the proverbial candy store, I read voraciously.

I re-examined the so-called messianic prophecies and became convinced Jesus could not have been the Messiah. Messiah was to regather Israel, end war and bring lasting peace. The New Testament claims Jesus is the savior but in Isaiah, God declares: "I am the Lord and beside me there is no savior" (43:11). Jehovah's Witnesses teach Jesus is subordinate to God. This had once appealed to my monotheistic leanings. Now, as I re-examined the New Testament, I realized Jehovah's Witnesses had misread it and that Jesus indeed is considered co-equal with God.

Until now, I had fed my *intellectual* hunger. But a new longing was developing – to associate and pray with other Jews. In the late fall of 1955, my cousin arranged to meet me outside Temple Israel for a late Friday evening Sabbath service. Arriving at the synagogue, I lingered nervously at the entrance, waiting for my cousin (the same cousin who had once upbraided me when I was witnessing on a street corner with the Watchtower.) Realizing she was late, I gathered courage and entered. The synagogue was strange to me, its grandeur a far cry from the humble Kingdom Hall I was accustomed to, or the modest down-town synagogue of my youth. Though surrounded by people, I felt strangely alone. I had been away too long. The ark was opened, revealing the Torah scrolls, resplendent in their velvet mantles and silver crowns. As the cantor intoned the *Mah Tovu* prayer – "How goodly are thy tents, O Jacob, thy tabernacles, O Israel" (the very words I had read sixteen years previous at my Bar-Mitzvah) – my feeling of estrangement subsided and was replaced by a rapturous joy such as I had never before experienced. The faith I had once been unable to find here, I had now found. After a fifteen-year sojourn in a strange land, I had come home.

(Footnote: In 1949, I had been giving a Sunday lecture at the Albany Kingdom Hall of Jehovah's Witnesses, on the corner of North Pearl Street and Livingston Avenue. A lovely lady had been invited to attend the lecture and I was introduced to her. Martha was a widow with two young children – Donald and Joyce. I mentored her in Jehovah's Witnesses, initiating her in the work. We married in 1951 and moved to East Greenbush, where I started a congregation. When I left Jehovah's Witnesses, Martha was willing to discuss the issue with me. We studied together and to my amazing good fortune, she joined me and converted to Judaism, along with her children Donald and Joyce. In 1956, our son Joel was born. We subsequently had a Jewish wedding. Martha became secretary in Temple Israel and then in the Hebrew Academy. She also was president of Hadassah and was highly esteemed and beloved. Donald and Joyce both attended Temple Israel Hebrew School, Jewish summer camps and were bar-and bat-mitzvah. Joel attended the Hebrew Academy.)

2

Letters to

Jewish Converts to Christianity

[*Recipients names have been changed for confidentiality.*]

Dear Sarah,
      I am deeply concerned over your recent inclination toward Christianity. I sense your involvement has a strong emotional element. You have been away from home and have received love and friendship from Christian friends, rendering you more susceptible to their missionary efforts. I myself once experienced what is transpiring in your life. In my youth, my maternal uncle who I loved and revered, came to me with the Christian message and won my heart. For fifteen years, from the age of fifteen to thirty, I was passionately committed to Christianity.

      When you attended my class, you challenged my remark that "contradictions in Judaism make it beautiful." As a Christian, I believed there can be no contradictions or unanswerable questions. We referred to our beliefs as the "Truth." All knowledge was given and vouchsafed by and through "God's elected channel." This was dogmatism and fundamentalism in the extreme. But what a precarious system this was, intended to satisfy those for whom everything is black and white! It fostered a child-like mentality that demands clear and unequivocal answers to every question. Mature persons know there are imponderables in life and no system has all the answers. For fifteen years I was content in believing every question has an answer – an answer that is indisputable.

To my good fortune, however, I was blessed with an inquiring mind, a passion for truth and insatiable curiosity – instincts that were to rescue me from my prison of mind-control. After fifteen years of passionate commitment to Christianity, I began to ask profound and searching questions which my mentors could not answer. When I subsequently found my way back to my ancestral heritage, it was as if the chains of my mind had been broken and my heart liberated. Once again I could breathe the fresh and invigorating air of independent and reasoned thinking. My dignity restored, I no longer had to conform to dogmatic opinions imposed by an unchallengeable authority. Words cannot describe my joy at being freed from the mental shackles which held me captive all those years. Even now, as a committed Jew, I continue to ask questions, to 'wrestle with God's angel,' like our father Jacob (Genesis 32:24-32). Father Abraham, the "friend of God," challenged God regarding Sodom (Genesis 18:25) and altered God's course of action! The Talmud is a massive monument to the freedom of dissent, where majority and minority opinions are recorded side by side. Yes, "contradictions in Judaism do make it beautiful." In Judaism, one is not perturbed and immobilized by contradictory points of view. Judaism grants a large measure of personal freedom – freedom of expression, the right of dissent and latitude of interpretation. Indeed, to question and challenge are hallmarks of Judaism. The New Testament, on the other hand, would discourage questioning in favor of childlike faith and meek submission (cf. Matthew 18:3, 4; 2 Timothy 2:33). Paul writes, "If any one preaches to you a gospel contrary to what you have received, let him be accursed" (Galatians 1:9). A religion that tolerates contradictions and remains viable is meritorious. On the other hand, Christianity stands or falls on Original Sin, Jesus as Messiah, Incarnation and Atonement. Remove any one of these dogmas and Christianity's raison d'être disappears. Without the belief in Original Sin, a "sacrificing redeemer" is irrelevant.

Sarah, you have a Jewish soul. Like most Jews, you are a liberal — a tendency stemming from fundamental premises in our religion. For example: "You shall love your neighbor as yourself (Leviticus 19:18); "You shall not oppress a stranger . . ." (Exodus 23:9); "The righteous gentiles have a share in the world to come" (Tosefta Sanhedrin 13). This liberalism, however, a precious stone in the crown of Judaism, sometimes proves our undoing. We are tolerant of other religions to the point of blurring differences and incompatibilities. Christianity, on the other, hand, espouses the doctrine of "exclusive salvation." Jesus said, "I am the way and the truth and the life; no one comes to the Father but through me" (John 14:6; cf. 3:36; I Timothy 25:5). This doctrine of exclusive salvation has been responsible for such heinous episodes as the crusades, inquisition, *auto-de-fe* and, finally, the holocaust. Martin Luther, father of the Reformation in Germany, was a rabid anti-Semite whose vicious diatribes against the Jews prepared the ground for Nazi Germany's "final solution." Hitler, a baptized Catholic, was never excommunicated by the Church. Judaism has no such doctrine of exclusive salvation. One need not be Jewish to be accepted by God: "He has showed you, O man, what is good and what the Lord requires of you, but to do justice, love kindness and walk humbly with your God" (Micah 6:8).

Sarah, you believe you are still Jewish because your Christian mentors have convinced you your belief in Jesus as messiah makes you a "completed Jew." This implies that Jews who do not accept Jesus as messiah are "incomplete." The dialectic that Jews who embrace Christ are "completed" Jews is a clever ploy, concocted by Christian missionaries to seduce Jews. Christianity is not Jewish; it is the antithesis of Judaism. To believe "God died on the cross" is not Jewish! The abrogation of the Torah is not Jewish! (See John 1:17; Galatians 3:24; Ephesians 2:15; Colossians 2:14). The New Testament, which is virulently anti-Jewish, is the source-book which has motivated faithful Christians throughout the centuries to persecute and kill Jewish "infidels." John has Jesus say to the "Jews" (not just a few Jewish miscreants): "You are of your father the devil and you do the will of your father. He was a murderer from the beginning . . ." (John 8:44). The Jews are called a "synagogue of Satan" (Revelation 2:9). John's use of the expression, "the Jews," is typically racist (John 1:19; 5:18; 6:41; 7:1,13; 8:22,37,38; 9:22; 19:7,12). The New Testament says the Jews willed their own annihilation: "And all the [Jews] answered, 'His blood be upon us and upon our children!'" (Matthew 27:26). *All* the Jews? This hateful, anti-Jewish canard surely contributed to the killing of six million Jews in Nazi Europe. Your Christian mentors will tell you those who conspired to kill the six million were not "true Christians." My answer is, "By their fruits you shall know them" (Matthew 7:16). What pains me is that the very document responsible for untold suffering to the Jewish people is now the source of your inspiration. Study the holocaust literature and read the testimonials of the Jewish survivors—their remarks about their "Christian" neighbors who betrayed them or were mute when Jews were herded onto cattle cars and taken away to the camps. Or read about the anti-Jewish vitriol preached from the Christian pulpits. My heart is broken when I see Jews embrace the teachings responsible for Jewish suffering without true knowledge of their implication.

When my uncle first preached Christianity to me, he prepared me for my family's opposition. My father, a Russian immigrant and son of a cantor, was a fiercely proud Jew who was intolerant of Christian missionaries. The Jews of Eastern

Europe had suffered much from anti-Semitism. My uncle quoted Matthew 10:36 and Luke 14:26: "A man's enemies shall be they of his own household. . . .If any one come to me and does not hate his own father and mother, he cannot be my disciple."

I know you have been given "evidence" that the Christian message preached to you must be of God because you received a "healing." Catholics claim "miraculous healings," as do Christian Scientists and adherents of eastern religions. And all these religious entities are in opposition to one another, each denying the other's validity. Judaism knows of divine healing. The second paragraph of the *amidah* says God "sustains life in his loving-kindness, upholds the fallen and heals the sick." The greater healing, however, comes from holding fast to the Torah, the "Tree of Life" (Proverbs 3:18).

Fundamental Christianity, as practiced in the charismatic Pentecostal churches, has powerful appeal and fascination, compared with the staid decorum of Jewish religious services. Judaism is a quiet faith, with little of the sensationalism and theatrics of the fundamental churches. Judaism listens to the "still small voice" (I Kings 19:11, 12), is less dogmatic, with less certainties and more questions. Moses asked God, "Please show me your glory"; to which God replied, "You cannot see my face . . ." (Exodus 33:18-23). Christianity would *visually* behold its god, like the ancient Israelites who demanded of Aaron, "Up, make us a god who shall go before us" (Exodus 32:1). Christianity claims it was necessary for God to materialize human flesh – the "Incarnation" – in order to save humanity. Judaism, however, is content with God's invisible presence: "Adonai is near to all who call upon him, to all who call upon him in truth" (Psalms 145:18). "I dwell in the high and holy place, and also with him who is of a contrite and humble spirit" (Isaiah 57:15; cf. Leviticus 26:11).

Yes, the exotic captivates, whereas "familiarity breeds

contempt." A shrewd salesman came to the door one day and little Jacob answered: The salesman began, "Son, I would like to buy those old, black, dented candlesticks on the mantel and I will give you these shiny, new candlesticks in exchange!" But something inside little Jacob said no. (The salesman's bright, new candlesticks were nickel-plated.)   Later, Jacob and his mother polished up the old silver candlesticks and they glowed brightly.   "But what about the dents?" asked Jacob. "They're all right," his mother replied. "Grandma and her mother before her lovingly kindled the Shabbat candles in them and sometimes they were dropped and were dented. But we still cherish them—even with the dents."

Shall we exchange our old, "tarnished" religion for a new, shiny one?   Or shall we study anew our old religion, removing the tarnish of ignorance so it glows brightly for us once more? And, oh those dents! They have a story to tell – of loving and long use. Yes, ours is an ancient religion – imperfect perhaps, but with a long and glorious history.

Why are Christians obsessed with converting Jews?   Is it because they believe they have something good to impart to us?   Or is it because of a certain insecurity which seeks validation from history's classic rejecter of Christianity? Why do Jews not share a similar passion for making converts? Persons of culture and intelligence can discuss differences without feeling frustration – content merely to be able to exchange views without needing total agreement.   But one who is insecure has an almost pathological need to obtain universal agreement.   Perhaps this partially explains Christianity's passion for making converts.

Christianity, begun by Jews, with strong Hebrew Scripture origins, may seem to have Jewish overtones.   But it has departed radically from biblical religion. The faith of Israel was uncompromisingly monotheistic: "I am the LORD your God . . . you shall have no other gods besides me" (Exodus 20:2, 3; cf. Deuteronomy 6:4 ;). Whereas God is "the first and the last" (Isaiah 44:6; 43:11), Jesus is called "the first and the last" (Revelation 2:8). Although Christianity claims to believe in "one" God, its belief in Jesus as god belies its claim (John 1:1). Christianity is disguised idolatry; the Trinity is a delusion. God's absolute oneness is the foundation of Hebrew faith.

Finally, as a Jew, I affirm the following: I believe in One God and repudiate the Trinity. I reject the Virgin Birth, Deity of Christ, Jesus as messiah, concept of Mediator and blood-atonement. I believe Messiah will be human. I believe in the eternalness of the Law Covenant and Israel as God's chosen people. I believe a Jew who accepts Jesus Christ as savior and messiah separates himself from the Jewish People.

Sarah, you have embraced Christianity without really knowing Judaism, our Holy Scriptures or the teachings of our Sages. You have given your heart to Christianity and repudiated your heritage. Tragically, history proves that Jewish converts to Christianity do not have Jewish grandchildren. My heart's desire is that you will return to your people, God's "own possession" (Exodus 19:5), whom He loves "with an everlasting love" (Jeremiah 31:3).

Dear Miriam,

I grieve for our people who have lost in you a precious soul – for our numbers are precariously few and diminishing. I know you still consider yourself Jewish, i.e., "Jewish-Christian." But Judaism and Christianity are incompatible. The word "Jew" is from Hebrew *Yehudah* – 'who praises Yah.' Your praise, ultimately, will be of Jesus, who will become the focus of your life. You will be nurtured by followers and lovers of Jesus and the New Testament will become your spiritual grazing ground. Among Messianic Jews, for example, one invariably encounters the expression, *B'shem Yeshua* – "In the name of Jesus." In their congregations one will not find the sacred Tetragrammaton JHVH but the words, "Yeshua, light of the world." No matter how strenuously Messianic Jews may protest otherwise, they acknowledge two gods (1 Corinthians 1:2, 3; 2 Corinthians 1:2: Galatians 1:3; Ephesians 1:2; and so through all the epistles.)

For Jews there is ONE God: "Hear, O Israel: Adonai is our God, Adonai is one. And you shall love Adonai your God with all your heart and with all your soul and with all your strength" (Deuteronomy 6:4, 5). This does not permit of the love of any other deity. We dare not twist these words into any other meaning, such as the spurious interpretation that God is a "compound unity" – "Father, son and holy spirit." It is written, "Take heed to yourselves lest your heart be deceived and you turn aside and serve other gods and worship them" (Deuteronomy 11:16). Jews still are susceptible to being led astray after alien religions. The prophet Isaiah declares unequivocally, "I am Adonai; that is my name. My glory will I not give to another" (42:8). Contrast this with John 1:14 and Revelation 5:12, where Jesus receives the glory. The Psalmist declares, "Blessed is Adonai Elohim, God of Israel, Who alone does wondrous things. And blessed is His glorious name for ever" (Psalms 72:18, 19). There are not *two* glorious names but one!

Whereas Christianity is Trinitarian and polytheistic, repudiating the absolute singularity and spirit-nature of God, Hebrew-biblical religion posits ONE GOD (Exodus 20:2, 3; Deuteronomy 4:39; Isaiah 43:11; 44:6, 8). Christianity rejects the eternal Torah (Law) of God (Romans 6:14; I Corinthians 9:20; Galatians 3:19, 24, 25; 5:18; Philippians 3:9). The Torah is eternal, never to be abrogated (Psalms 111:9; Exodus 31:16, 17). The Torah is life-giving (Leviticus 18:5; Deuteronomy 32:46, 47; 30:6, 8; 5:33; Psalms 119:92, 93, Proverbs 3:18). In

Christianity, God is accessible only through Jesus (John 14:6). In Hebrew-biblical religion, God is directly accessible (Psalms 145:18).   In Christianity, the covenant between God and Israel has been abrogated whereas the covenant with Israel was eternal (Deuteronomy 29:29).   In Christianity, salvation is through faith in Jesus and his sacrifice.   In Hebrew-biblical religion, salvation is based on repentance and right conduct (Isaiah 1:16--18).

You claim 'your relationship is sealed by the Holy Spirit through the blood of his son Jesus Christ.' This is not Jewish but pagan.   Human sacrifice is repugnant to God (Leviticus 18:21; 20:2-15; Deuteronomy 12:31; 18:10; 2 Kings 3:26, 27; Jeremiah 19:4,5; Psalms 106:37,38; Hosea 6:6). Atonement is through righteous deeds (Proverbs 16:6; 21:3; Psalms 51:14-17; 40:6; 1 Samuel 15:22; Micah 6:6-8; Isaiah 1:11-18; Ezekiel 18:5-9; Exodus 32:30-33).

You said 'you have met many religious Jews and rabbis who follow the letter of the Law, yet the Law is not written on their hearts.'   Only God can know what is written on one's heart.   Outward appearances do not always signal what is within (1 Samuel 16:17).   It is true Jews are demonstrative about their religion, practicing many rituals and ceremonies. But outward practice does not preclude inwardness. You state our discussion 'awakened in you a renewed love and hope for your people Israel.' The Church has "loved" the Jewish People for two thousand years, seeking to convert Jews to Christ.   But this love has been death for the Jewish People. A Jew who converts to Christianity is a Jew lost to his people. Millions of Jews have been absorbed into the Christian fold. Where are their descendants?   It is even possible, that among the murderers of Jewish men, women and children in Nazi Germany, there were descendants of Jewish converts to Christianity. What a heart-wrenching thought!

You state: "I could flood you with scriptures that support the messiaship of Jesus."   Miriam, the New Testament was written to prove Jesus was the Messiah. The writers cleverly matched the life and death of Jesus to quotations from the Hebrew Scriptures. It is like an archer who shoots an arrow and then draws a target around the arrow to prove his marksmanship. Setting scripture alongside scripture to authenticate Jesus – as the "red-letter" Bibles do – is naive. The writers of the New Testament made out a very good case for Jesus but one thing they could not do: The promised Messiah was to bring peace and establish an everlasting kingdom (Isaiah 9:6,7). Jesus did neither.

The prayer which Jesus taught his followers on the mount (Matthew 6:9-13) is remarkable and most instructive: *"Our* Father," not "My Father." God is the Father of us all (Malachi 2:10). "Who is in heaven" -- The Father is in heaven, never to materialize, never to be seen, only to be apprehended with the eye of faith (Exodus 33:20; II Chronicles 6:18; Isaiah 66:1; John 4:24). "Your kingdom come" – The kingdom of God is yet to come. "Your will be done on earth" – His will is not yet done on earth. The universal fulfillment of God's will on earth is one of the evidences of Messiah's coming. Because evil yet reigns, Jews cannot believe Jesus was the Messiah (Isaiah 9:7). "Forgive us our sins" – God alone forgives sins. No mediator is needed (II Chronicles 6:36--39). "For *yours* is the kingdom" – The kingdom is God's exclusively. Indeed, the prayer of Jesus is a prayer any Jew can pray. It is wholly a Jewish prayer!

Miriam, you need to know, that if you persist in your chosen course, you and your descendants surely will be lost to your people. From earliest times, Jews who have embraced Christianity have disappeared and left no Jewish descendants. You are laboring in a stranger's vineyard (Songs 1:6). Until you return to the vineyard of the God of Israel and labor alongside his people, your soul will never be fully at peace. I once labored in a stranger's vineyard and never attained quietness of soul until I returned to my father's house.

[Postscript: To the reader: There are several principles to keep in mind when dealing with Jews who have left Judaism. One should not be overly sanguine about winning a Jew back. Jews are a "stubborn people" (Exodus 32:9). A Jew who has committed to another religion tends to hold fast to it and excel. Nonetheless, we are duty-bound to try to win them back. We are taught in **Pirke Avot,** *"Know how to answer an apostate" (2:19). That is why I wrote my book,* **Make Us a God.** *One should not be confrontational but follow Hillel's advice: "Loving God's creatures and drawing them close to the Torah"* (**Pirke Avot** *1:12). We are taught, "He who saves a single soul saves a whole world" (Sanhedrin 38a). He who restores one Jewish soul to his people is as though he had saved generations of Jews.]*

3

Judaism Is More Than Ritual;
It Is a Way of Life

In the seventies, I had an encounter with a former student. Chaim was a quiet, sensitive, thoughtful young man, with deep spiritual needs. Several years prior to our meeting, he had opted out of Judaism and affiliated with a Hebrew-Christian missionary group. I met with Chaim and invited him to share his feelings about Judaism. Among his responses were the all-to-familiar ones: Judaism is a body without a soul involving empty ritual. Synagogue attendance is a rote experience, devoid of feeling and spirituality. In a succeeding essay, I will go into more detail about my dialogue with Chaim.

Judaism is more than ritual. It is a way of life. It is a viable religion. By "viable," we mean, within human capability – answering basic human needs, as the Torah teaches: "For the commandment which I command you this day is not too hard you . . . it is in your mouth and in your heart, so that you can do it" (Deuteronomy 30:11-14).

The word "viable" is from the Latin *vita, 'life.'* Judaism is focused on life. By contrast, the New Testament posits a morbid view of man as depraved and irretrievable except by vicarious atonement (Romans 5:12). With its focus on the crucified Jesus, Christianity is obsessed with death. Witness the phenomenal interest in the movie, "The Passion of Christ." Whereas the most common amulet of Judaism is

25

the *mezuzah*, containing the Scripture about loving God, the most common amulet of Christianity is the crucifix, whose motif is death (cf. I Corinthians 2:2; Philippians 1:21--23; Romans 7:24).

With its abnormal obsession with death and the next world, the church sought to justify the stake-burnings of Jewish "infidels" by appealing to the New Testament scripture: "You are to deliver this man to Satan for the destruction of the flesh, that his spirit may be saved in the day of the Lord Jesus" (I Corinthians 5:5). And, remarkably this was called *auto-de-fe,* 'act of faith'! It was considered meritorious to kill the "sinful" Jew to save his soul!

Judaism is not burdened with the morbid view of depraved man, as taught in the New Testament. Judaism teaches: "The soul which you have given me is pure." Genesis 9:6 declares: "God made man in his own image." This, we should note, was *after* Eden. Adam's transgression did not change man's God-like image. "Original Sin" is not a Jewish teaching.

Although Judaism contains mystical elements, essentially it is reasonable, sane and balanced, discouraging extremism. Judaism is a way of *Life*. It does not impose demands contrary to nature. Asceticism – self-denial – is not a Jewish ideal. Rabbi Yose taught: "One may not mortify oneself by (excessive) fasting . . . Rabbi Judah said in the name of Rav: What is Rabbi Yose's reason? Because in saying, 'And man became a living soul' (Genesis 2:7), Scripture means: Keep alive the soul I have given you" (Taanit 25). Compare Jesus' saying: "If any man would come after me, let him deny himself and take up his cross and follow me" (Matthew 16:24).

In Judaism, sustaining life takes precedence over ritual: "Saving life pre-empts Sabbath observance" (Yoma 50). There are religious groups that place ritual above life. Jehovah's Witnesses, for example, prohibit blood-transfusion, even when life is at stake. But Judaism teaches: "You shall therefore keep my statutes and my ordinances, by doing which *a man shall live"* (Leviticus 18:5). And the rabbis add, "and not die." Asceticism is not a Jewish ideal: "In the future, one shall give an account for everything his eye beheld and he did not eat" (Jerus. Sotah 3:4).

While Judaism encourages the enjoyment of life's legitimate pleasures, it discourages hedonism—extreme self-gratification. It seeks to balance this with obligation— mitzvah. Hillel taught: "If I am not for myself, who will be for me; but if I am only for myself, what am I?" (Pirke Avot 1:4). This is Judaism's sane balance between self and social obligation.

[Below are some core values of Judaism which contribute to the enhancement of life. References not specified refer to Pirke Avot—a tractate of the Talmud]

PRE-EMINENCE OF LEARNING

There are different genres of learning: Germany was renown for its universities and for having more PhD's per-capita than any other country. But Germany was host to history's most heinous crime again humanity—the Holocaust. The study of science and the arts does not necessarily humanize its patrons.

There is another kind of learning: Moral education. The sense of right and wrong is not instinctive. Man is not innately ethical. The natural instincts are survival and predation, not altruism. The conscience needs to be educated. Rabbi Shimon the Righteous taught that one of the three pillars of the world is Torah (moral instruction). We are also taught, "If you have learned much Torah, do not congratulate yourself, for you were created for this" (2:9). The American commitment to a balanced, nutritious diet is well known. What is often lacking, however, is the nourishment of the soul. The spiritual vitality of a Jewish community can be measured by its level of Judaic knowledge. Rabban Elazar ben Azariah taught: "If there is no Torah, there is no *derech eretz* [ethical behavior]" (3:21). Character must be instilled.

The "pious ignoramus" has no place in Judaism. Hillel taught: "... an unlearned person cannot be pious" (2:6). This is not elitism but an acknowledgement that conscience needs to be molded by good teaching. True religion is doing the right thing. The prophet Micah taught that the requirements of true religion were justice and mercy. This is the goal of Torah-education. In Judaism, this genre of education is pre-eminent.

LEARNING AND DOING

Shimon ben Gamliel taught: "Learning is not the principle thing but doing" (1:17). In a community of scholars, this needed to be said. Learning—and only learning—can be a fetish. For those so inclined, it can provide abundant pleasure. But learning not accompanied by deeds is empty. Rabbi Hanina ben Dosa taught: "He whose wisdom is greater than his deeds, his wisdom does not endure" (3:12).

HUMILITY INCREASES LEARNING

Ben Zoma taught: "Who is wise? He who learns from everyone" (4:1). This requires humility. The conceited person arrogantly dismisses other opinions or chafes at correction. The wise person is not offended when corrected. Proverbs 12:1 admonishes: "Teach a wise man and he will be yet wiser."

LEARNING AND TEACHERS

Jose ben Joezer of Zerodah taught: "Let your house be a meeting place for the sages and sit in the dust of their feet and drink in their words with thirst" (1:4). Yehoshuah ben Perachia taught: "Provide yourself with a teacher" (1:6). The primacy of education in Judaism is enunciated in the very first line of Pirke Avot: "Raise up many students" (1:1).

JUSTICE

Judges are counseled: "Be deliberate in judgment" (1:1)—Weigh all the evidence and do not rush to judgment. Yehoshuah ben Perachia taught: "Judge every one in the scale of merit" (1:6) – Seek out the good in people rather than focus on their weaknesses. Hillel taught: "Judge not your fellow man until you have been in his place" (2:5). Rabbi Meir taught: "Look not upon the container but at what is in it" (4:27) – Avoid stereotyping. Ben Azzi taught: "Do not despise any person" (4:3) – The unwarranted rejection of others is often motivated by the predatory instinct. Controlling this inclination is one of the purposes of Torah-education.

HONORING HUMANKIND

Rabbi Eliezer taught: "Let the honor of your fellow man be as dear to you as your own" (2:15). Rabbi Elazar Hamodai taught: "He who shames his fellow man in public . . . has no share in the world to come" (3:15). This is an expansion of, "Love your neighbor as yourself."

SELF-RESPECT

The rabbis were aware of the harmful effects of excessive self-criticism and feelings of worthlessness: "Be not evil in your own eyes" (2:18). Judaism has a formula for looking outward and not obsessing on one's inadequacies. It is a life of mitzvot involving acts of loving-kindness.

A GOOD NAME

Rabbi Shimon taught: "There are three crowns: The crown of Torah, the crown of priesthood and the crown of royalty. But the crown of a good name excels them all" (4:17). Hillel taught: "A name made great is a name destroyed" (1:13). He was referring to fame sought by unethical means—another manifestation of the predatory instinct. In a similar vein, the

rabbis teach, "He who pursues honor, honor flees from him."
Ben Zoma taught: "Who is worthy of honor? He who
honors others" (4:1).

The "Me" generation says: "I don't care what others
think. I do as I please." Yehudah Hanasi taught: "What
is the right course one should choose? That which is an
honor to him and brings him honor from others" (2:1). This
is an example of balance in Judaism. But it works only in
a righteous environment, not a criminal one. At times, one
may need to swim against the tide. In such an event, we
follow the teaching of Nittai the Arbelite: "Keep far from an
evil companion" (1:7).

RESPONSIBILITY

When others shirk their responsibility, we must fill the void.
Hillel taught: "In a place where there are no men, endeavor
to be a man" (2:6). Scholars may incline to remain aloof and
avoid leadership. This void surely will be filled—by villains
and fools. We are familiar with the complaint which begins
with, "Why don't *they*..." We are the *they!*

PEACE

Hillel taught: "Be of the disciples of Aaron, loving peace
and pursuing peace, loving our fellow creatures and drawing
them close to the Torah" (1:12). It is not preaching but caring
that inspires others to lives of goodness. Rabbi Matityah ben
Heresh taught: "Be the first to greet everyone with shalom"
(4:20). Rabbi Hanina ben Dosa taught: "He in whom the
spirit of mankind finds pleasure, the spirit of the All-present
finds pleasure" (3:13). An attribute of valid religion is the
spirit of inclusiveness. Hillel taught: "Do not separate from
the community" (2:5).

THE POOR

Jose ben Yohanan taught: "Let your house be open wide and let the poor be members of your household" (1:5). Maimonides taught: Employ the poor. A praiseworthy trait of the rich and powerful is their compassion for the poor and helpless.

INTEGRITY

"Be as diligent regarding a light commandment as with a weighty one" (2:1). This can be extended beyond religious obligations to all of life's tasks. Character is measured by the little things we do. Rabbi Tarfon taught: "It is not yours to complete the work; neither are you free to desist from it" (2:21) "Nobody made a greater mistake than he who did nothing because he could only do a little" (author unknown).

WORK

"Love work and hate lordship" (1:10). Menial labor is not dishonorable. This evidently was directed toward scholars. Shunning "lordship" does not mean refusing leadership when one is called upon and is qualified. But a leader should not be arbitrary and oppressive but lead by example and understanding.

Above, we have shared some of the wisdom of the Jewish Sages, leading to a more meaningful and responsible life. Indeed, Judaism is more than ritual; *it is a way of life.*

4

Historic Awareness—
Key to Jewish Survival

The approximate numbers of the world's major religions are: Christian—2.1 billion; Muslim—1.2 billion; Hindu—900 million; Buddhist—376 million; Jews—14 million. What is striking about this table? As an ancient people, the number of world Jewry should be vastly higher! Truly, we are an "endangered species." Jewish attrition due to a low birth rate is beyond our control. But Jewish apathy and Jewish conversions to pseudo Jewish cults, such as "Jews for Jesus" and "Messianic Judaism," are issues we need to address.

We are taught, "Whoever is engaged with the Book of Exodus is a though he had stood at Mount Sinai" (Seder Arakim in K'bod Huppah 19a). [Note the word *engaged*, for we shall return to it later.] Why such high praise for the Book of Exodus? Because it recounts the physical and spiritual genesis of the Jewish People—nationhood and Torah. The Passover Haggada states: "It is a mitzvah to recount the exodus from Egypt. He who elaborates on the exodus from Egypt is praiseworthy." We are further taught: "In every generation one should imagine that he went out of Egypt." "Thus," writes Menachem Kasher, "the spirit of freedom ever remains in the heart of the Jew, even in the harshest periods of exile and persecution."

Whereas Israel's exodus from Egypt marked the physical

birth of the nation of Israel, Sinai marked its spiritual birth. And just as we must imagine ourselves as among the freed Israelite slaves, so must we stand with our ancestors at Sinai. This is alluded to in Deuteronomy 29:14, 15: "These are the words of the covenant which the Lord commanded Moses to make with the people of Israel . . . You stand this day all of you before the Lord your God . . . Nor is it with you only I make this sworn covenant, but *with him who is not here with us this day [Italics added] . . . .*" What is the lesson here? Historic awareness is the key to Jewish survival.

Judaism is a fragile entity. To survive as Jews in a pluralistic society is a constant challenge, especially since Jews are by nature inquisitive and respectful of other cultures. Jews may disassociate from Judaism out of apathy. But, more seriously, Jews embrace other cultures, religions, sects and cults. How, for example, shall we win back a Jew who has joined "Jews for Jesus" or "Messianic Judaism"—entities that are so seductive because they are *pseudo*-Jewish? Shall we engage in scriptural debate? In exceptional cases, this may succeed. But experience has shown this method often is fruitless.

This author's book, "Make Us a God," based on years of research, contains copious scriptural arguments to counter the "Hebrew Christians." One would hope it would be eminently successful in bringing Jews back, especially since its author was a Christian who returned to Judaism. But, unfortunately, it is not that simple.

Recently this book was provided to a young Jewish collegian who had embraced Christianity. When the student's mother was asked if the book had been read, the reply was, "She has perused it and thinks she has answers." Based on years of experience, this author is not so sanguine as to think this thoroughly researched polemic will turn the young woman's heart back to Judaism.

Above we quoted the dictum, "He who is engaged in

the Book of Exodus is as though he stood at Mount Sinai."
History! History! Jews abandon their heritage because they
do not know it. To know the Jewish heritage is to be proud
and to be dedicated to its preservation and perpetuation. To
stand at Sinai is to feel the passion and fervor of our ancestors
as they stood before the quaking, burning, mountain, amidst
thunder and lightning and the ear-shattering blasts of the
rams' horns. This provides the strength and courage to
remain proudly Jewish.

More than knowing our history, however, is to participate
in its re-enactment. This is how we truly stand with our
ancestors. When we kindle the Sabbath lights, we stand
with our ancestors. When we re-enact the Exodus in the
Passover Seder, we stand with our ancestors. When we sit
in booths on Sukkot, we dwell with our ancestors during
their wilderness sojourn. When we celebrate the Festival of
Shavuot, we stand with our ancestors at Sinai to receive the
Torah. History and Re-enactment!

Recently the mother of a young woman who had
embraced Christianity remarked: "But my daughter feels she
still is Jewish!" Yes, ethnically, she is Jewish. But will her
children and grandchildren be Jewish? Using the metaphor
of a bottle of wine and a bottle of water – Judaism is the
wine; Christianity the water. We mix the two and the liquid
retains the wine-color. We mix them again and the wine-
color is barely visible. So we start out with a Jew who has
converted to Christianity but claims still to be Jewish. The
convert's children have a diluted identity as Jews and the
grandchildren have almost none.

We quote again: "He who is engaged in the book of
Exodus is as though he had stood at Sinai." This passage
doesn't say, 'He who *studies* the book of Exodus' but, "he who
is *engaged* in the book of Exodus." To be *engaged* in the book
of Exodus is to *re-enact* the historic experience of our people.
Knowing and celebrating Jewish history through ritual and

festival –observance instills pride of heritage and strengthens linkage with our ancestors. It is a strong deterrent to Jewish apathy and attrition and a key to Jewish survival.

5

Is Judaism a Body without a Soul?

In a previous essay, we spoke about Chaim, my former student, who left Judaism and joined a Hebrew-Christian missionary group. Chaim claimed synagogue attendance is a rote experience, devoid of spirituality and Judaism is a "body without a soul."

As a youngster, I had heard a similar remark from my maternal uncle who had abandoned Judaism for a Christian sect. He criticized the recitation of prayers in an unintelligible tongue. In my youthful naiveté, this sounded convincing and I had no answer.

Years later, having had a renaissance with Judaism and returning to the synagogue after a long absence, I found myself praying in Hebrew from the Jewish prayer book – repeating words whose meaning I did not understand. This troubled me. I recalled my uncle's criticism about meaningless prayer in an unintelligible tongue and I vowed to set about learning our ancient language. At first, it wasn't easy. But should it be? Consider how assiduously we apply ourselves to mastering secular disciplines to prepare for a career. Should not our heritage demand similar devotion and energy? I eventually mastered our sacred tongue and was able to understand the ancient Hebrew prayers of our people.

In my discussion with Chaim, I suggested that sitting in judgment of Jews in the synagogue is presumptuous and ill-considered. While it is true on certain holidays Jews throng to the synagogue who rarely attend the rest of the year, I do not judge their motives—whether or not they are having a spiritual experience.

My discussion with Chaim reminded me of a drama that had occurred during a morning synagogue service. An elderly gentleman was praying in the mechanical style of one accustomed to repeating the same prayers since his youth. His eyes never lowered to the pages of his prayer book. As I watched him devoutly reciting the prayers from memory, respect welled up within me for one who had been faithful to his heritage for a lifetime. I was transported to another time, perhaps a little *shtetel* in Europe, where I envisioned a little boy sitting next to his father in the synagogue, learning the prayers by rote.

Judaism indeed invites encounter with God: "Adonai is near to all who call upon Him. . ." (Psalms 145:18). This is from the prayer *Ashrei,* which is chanted daily in the synagogue. A key word in the Jewish religious vocabulary is *kavannah* – 'direction, intention.' As applied to prayer, it means sincere, thoughtful prayer. Pirke Avot admonishes, "When you pray, do not make your prayer mechanical [Heb. *kevah*]" (2:18) – Do not race thoughtlessly over the words. In commenting on this, the Talmud in tractate Berachot asks: "What is meant by *kevah?* – Whoever is unable to add something new." One is encouraged to depart from the fixed text to express a personal thought or seek new meaning in the oft-repeated words. Meaningful prayer is advocated and valued in Judaism.

Yes, Judaism has many rituals—Shabbat candles, Tefillin, Succah, the Pesach Seder and the Lulav and Etrog. It is easy for an unfriendly critic to point to these and accuse Jews of meaningless ritual. But such accusations smack of self-righteousness. Christianity has its rituals as well and its worshipers certainly are not immune from perfunctory prayer and practice. Non-Jews are no better or worse than Jews in this regard. Ritual, by its very nature of repetitiveness, is subject to becoming perfunctory, whether in the synagogue or in the church.

As good teachers, our sages recognized ideas are not transmitted in a vacuum. So they devised ingenious audio-visuals—rituals to embody the ideas of Judaism. Just as music is played on instruments, ritual embodies concepts. Indeed, it can be demonstrated that the intention of Jewish ritual is to humanize. The Psalmist wrote, "The word of Adonai is refined [pure]" (Psalms 18:30). Every ritual has an inner meaning. It is but for us to discern it and translate it into worthy deeds

Consider two prominent examples of Jewish ritual – The Sabbath and the dietary laws. Abraham Joshua Heschel describes the Sabbath as "a day of armistice in the economic struggle with our fellow men and the forces of nature." The Sabbath is a time for getting in touch with ourselves, our families and our friends. The Jewish dietary laws have an ethical dimension. The slaughtered animal is not to be bruised, injured or mutilated. The death-stroke is to be swift, with minimal pain to the animal. The value concept is *tsa-ar ba-alei chaim* – '**compassion** for creature life.' The Torah teaches: "You shall not boil a kid in its mother's milk" (Deuteronomy 14:21). The separation of meat and dairy products conveys a sensitive regard for creature-life and an avoidance of barbarism. The limiting of animal-species as food-sources diminishes the tendency toward voraciousness and gluttony.

When young Jews like Chaim are turned off, we should not hasten to blame the synagogue or Judaism. Of course, we need to be sensitive to the synagogue's shortcomings and always seek for more meaningfulness. However, unless one comes to the synagogue with the right disposition, it places too big a burden on the synagogue to expect it to perform spiritual wonders. One cannot cut down a tree and use the green wood in a fireplace. The wood must be seasoned. Where and how does the seasoning take place that prepares one for the synagogue? In the home. Judaism is a home-oriented religion. Pious Jews pray at home. One of the most memorable images I retain from my childhood is of my grandfather putting on Tefillin in the morning and reciting the morning prayers. Another unforgettable memory is that of my grandmother kindling the Sabbath candles. How could I ever forget the warm glow of those candles in the silver candlesticks and the look of serenity and love on my grandmother's face! These memories created "homing" instincts which, although I was to stray from Judaism, enabled me in later years to be drawn back to my heritage.

Indeed, the soul of Judaism is fashioned in the home. It is here the warmth of Judaism is created and transmitted—where the sparks of Judaism are ignited in the hearts of children. When a child sees his mother light the Sabbath candles, his father bless mother and the children, the family join hands for *Shalom Aleichem*, his father recite Kiddush, bless the challah loaves and recite the blessings after the meal—when a child witnesses and experiences these—here is the soul of Judaism. Here is the fire whose embers will glow forever.

Children are most affected by what their parents do—not by what they preach. The Jewish deeds of parents bear witness to their devotion to Judaism. How pleasant in the hearts and minds of children are the words of parents whose deeds are consistent with their words.

When Chaim talked about not finding the soul in Judaism, I believe he was thinking of religious experiences—fervor, awe, the mystical and emotionalism. These are evident in Christian Pentecostalism. Pentecostals once were called "holy rollers" because they would sometimes fall to the floor in a religious frenzy, uttering unintelligible sounds called "speaking in tongues." We do not deny that fervor and awe are legitimate religious emotions that lift the spirit and act as a spiritual anti-depressant. But, in a Jewish framework, "soul" has a meaning more profound than the mystical, transcendent religious experience we have alluded to. The Torah is a "Tree of Life" (Proverbs 3:18). The soul of Judaism is the Torah. The essence of the Torah, as taught by Rabbi Akivah, is, "You shall love your neighbor as yourself" (Leviticus 19:18). We read further in Leviticus: "You shall keep my statutes and ordinances which, if one does them, he shall live by them" (18:5). The essence of "soul" in Judaism is the enhancement and sustaining of life. "The mitzvot [the Torah's commandments] were given to purify us" (Rav, Tanhuma shemini) – to ennoble and make us more fully human. This is the essential soul of Judaism. This was my message to the young Jew Chaim. Perhaps, some day, his eyes will be opened, as were mine, to behold the spiritual greatness that is the soul of Judaism.

6

Whose Torah Is Living?

I had a telephone conversation with the wife of the "rabbi" of the local "messianic" congregation. ("Messianic Judaism" is an updated version of "Jews for Jesus" – fundamental Christianity with a Jewish veneer. Services are held on Friday evening, with *kippot* [yarlmekahs], *talitot* [Jewish prayer shawls], a Torah scroll and Israeli-style music and dancing.) My conversation went something like this: ("R"=rabbi's wife.)

R: Chaim, an awesome event happened in the congregation last night! Someone plaited a wreath of thorns to put on the Torah. The congregation was swept away! Chaim, it was awesome!

C: You mean . . . like the crown of thorns they supposedly put on Jesus?

R: Yes, Chaim. It was awesome! The Torah is the embodiment of Yeshua. He is the living word of God!

C: You know, on the festival of Shavuot, we put wreaths of evergreen branches on three of our Torah scrolls

R: That's awesome! *Three* scrolls! You know what that symbolizes! (She was alluding to the Trinity.)

C: You have missed the real significance. You have focused

on the pagan, polytheistic Christian doctrine of the Trinity but have completely overlooked the deeper significance. You put a wreath of thorns on your Torah – dead thorns, thorns that are sharp and piercing, that wound and cause pain. We use living branches of the evergreen because for Jews the Torah is a "Tree of Life," which has sustained the Jewish People for millennia. Your god died. Our God is *El Chai v'Kayam,* the eternal, living God. For you the Torah is death-dealing, as Paul said: "The commandment which promised life proved to be death" (Romans 7:4, 10). Jews who embrace "Messianic Judaism," despite its Jewish trappings, are lost to their people. Yes, the thorn-wreath on your Torah scroll is a powerful symbol that, although you have the body – the "Jewish" externals – you do not have the *living* soul. The Torah can only live and impart life in an authentic Jewish environment. It is not a living entity in a "Messianic" congregation.

7

"Messianic" Wedding

I attended a "Messianic" wedding. (As I have explained elsewhere, "Messianic Judaism" is a "modern" version of "Jews for Jesus" — fundamental Christianity along "Pentecostal" lines with Jewish trappings.) Expecting the wedding to be held in a "messianic synagogue," I was surprised to learn it would take place in a church. Surprised — but not completely — for I do not believe in the much-touted "Jewishness" of "Messianic Jews." While I do not question their right to hold their ceremony wherever they choose, I am calling attention to the serious flaw in their proclaimed Jewishness.

Yes, there was a *chupah* (traditional Jewish wedding canopy); but how incongruous it was in front of a large, bold cross! The canopy partly obscured the cross — partly but not completely. I thought of the symbolism: "Messianic Judaism" would obscure its Christian character but cannot do so completely. Its Christian nature shows through!

The bride and groom did not stand *under* the wedding canopy but *in front* of it — more symbolism: "Messianic Jews" stand *outside* the House of Israel but have not entered. They affect the symbols of Judaism but do not have the spirit and soul of Judaism.

The ceremony began with the recitation of a *b'rachah* (Hebrew blessing). As the blessing was begun, I thought, "Something Jewish!" To my dismay, however, though the blessing was couched in Hebrew, the words were Christian: "Blessed are thou, O Lord our God . . . who has sanctified us in the blood of Jesus, the light of the world."

I waited in vain for the groom to break the glass – a traditional Jewish custom concluding the wedding ceremony to symbolize sorrow over the destruction of the Temple. Instead, the bride and groom partook of Christian Communion – participation in the body and blood of Christ. The only *kippah* in the congregation was mine!

While I wish the bride and groom every happiness, I do not believe they will have Jewish grandchildren.

8

Synagogue President Converts to Messianic Judaism

[The following is an excerpt from a letter to the Jewish newspaper Forward, concerning the president of a Utica synagogue who converted to "Messianic Judaism."]

I recently had occasion to discuss this issue with a leader of the Albany "Messianic" congregation, which, incidentally, the gentleman from Utica attends. I asked her, "What if the Jewish community *did* recognize and accept Messianic Jews? How would it play out?" She replied, "There would be a sharing that would redound to our mutual benefit." I pressed her and said, "Don't you mean you would endeavor to win Jews to Christ – in short, missionize Jews?" She hedged and said she doesn't like to use the word "missionize." When I asked her if she lights the Sabbath candles, she said yes. When I asked what blessing she recites, she replied she uses the traditional Jewish prayer and after the words, *v'tsivanu l'hadlik ner shel Shabbat* – "who has commanded us to kindle the Sabbath lights" – she appends the words, *b'dam yeshua or ha-olam* -- "in the blood of Jesus, light of the world."

Messianic Jews passionately protest their exclusion from the Jewish community. Their literature constantly inveighs against the "injustice" of not being recognized as Jews. A. G. Fruchtenbaum writes: "[The Hebrew Christian] considers himself a member of the Jewish community but is not considered one by his fellow Jews. He is extremely loyal to the Jews and yet is considered by them to be a traitor" (*Hebrew Christianity*, p. 59).

Upon reading the above, I wrote the following in the margin of my book: "But Hebrew Christians call Jews 'unbelievers' [ibid. p. 107] so that, in actuality, *they have separated themselves from us!*" Indeed, this accords with John's statement: "He who does not obey the Son shall not see life but the wrath of God rests upon him" (John 3:36). Fruchtenbaum continues: "The basic cause of Jewish suffering is their disobedience to the revealed will of God and unbelief in the person of the Messiah" (ibid. p. 80). In effect, Fruchtenbaum is saying the Holocaust was a punishment from God for Jewish unbelief! Could the Synagogue welcome into its midst one who holds this conviction? Fruchtenbaum asks: "Do Hebrew Christians believe differently from Gentile Christians? Regarding the basic doctrines of the Christian Faith, the answer is no." Regarding the Torah, Fruchtenbaum writes: "The Law of Moses, especially as represented by the Ten Commandments, is a ministration of death and . . . condemnation" (ibid. p. 85).

The question whether a Jewish believer in Jesus is a Jew is analogous to the question concerning the "Jewishness" of Jesus. There is no question that Jesus was born to a Jewish mother. The critical issue for Jews is not his birth but the religion that developed around him after his death. It is that religion that has profoundly affected the Jewish people and their history. Belief *is* crucial because belief affects behavior. A Jewish believer in Jesus, with all the encumbrances of his Christian beliefs, in a Jewish congregation and in a Jewish community, would not be salutary for Jews.

"Messianic Jews" claim they share a commitment to the survival of the Jewish people and should be entitled to all the privileges of being a Jew. This notwithstanding, it is undeniable that the goal of "Messianic Judaism" – and all evangelical Christians – is *the ultimate conversion of the Jews.* Conversion has invariably meant annihilation for Jews. Jewish converts to Christianity do not have Jewish grandchildren. The premise of the missionary is that Christianity is the true religion and those who do not embrace Christianity are eternally damned. This is immoral.

I uphold the decision of the Utica congregation to deny leadership to the individual in question. Let him worship in their synagogue, if he so desires – although I believe, in time, if he is faithful to his Christian beliefs, he will remove himself – or, God willing, return to the Covenant of Israel.

9

Mel Gibson's Movie,
The Passion of Christ

Tucked away on the last page of "The Jewish World" of February 12, 2004, was a small paragraph about Mel Gibson's new movie, "The Passion of Christ." Relegating this to the back of the paper seems to suggest this movie-event was of minor significance. It may, however, prove to be of monumental significance to Jews.

Newsweek thinks so. The bloodied visage of actor-portrayed Jesus wearing a crown of thorns stares out at us on the cover of the February 16 issue and the title screams: "Who Really Killed Jesus?" Advance sales are soaring as Evangelical congregations buy up showings. Gibson's film is expected to gross upwards of $30 million in the first five days and be viewed by millions as the most watched passion play in history. Upon viewing the film, the Pope said, "It is as it was." Billy Graham wept after seeing it.

Commenting on the movie's being a literal rendition of the New Testament account, Newsweek notes this is problematic: "The New Testament is not always historically accurate, having been penned long after the purported events took place." "The roots of anti-Semitism," writes Newsweek, "lie in overly literal readings . . . of New Testament texts . . . . When the Gospel authors implicated 'the Jews' in Jesus' passion . . . the writers had a very specific group in mind: the Temple Elite . . . . By 'the Jews,' the writers did not mean all Jewish people then and in the future. They meant the "Temple elite." "Temple Elite" is Newsweek's euphemism for the Jewish spiritual leaders – the rabbis, if you will.

But this interpretation is questionable. If John had meant the "Temple leaders," he could have said, "The priests, scribes and Pharisees," as did Matthew, Mark and Luke. When the New Testament means the "Temple Elite," it singles them out. When John says, "the Jews," he means the Jews. Through the ages, when Christian believers read "the Jews," it is clear what they understood it to mean.

Matthew has the Jews viciously clamoring for Jesus' crucifixion: "Pilate . . . took water and washed his hands before the crowd [not just the Jewish elite], saying, 'I am innocent of this man's blood; see to it yourselves.' And all the people answered, 'His blood be on us and our children' "(Matthew 27:24, ff.) Under pressure, Gibson cut this passage from his film.

A rabbi and Christian pastor were discussing the Gibson film on television. When the rabbi expressed his apprehensions about the film, the pastor assured the rabbi, "Whenever we talk about the Crucifixion, we always say, 'Christ died on the Roman cross.'" But let us not be too comforted by this. When the Christian reads the New Testament, he encounters the words of Paul to the Thessalonians: "You suffered the same things from your own countrymen as they did from the Jews, who killed both the Lord Jesus and the prophets and drove us out, and displease God and oppose all men . . . But God's wrath has come upon them at last" (I Thessalonians 2:14). And this, from the Jew Paul!

It is written in the book of Acts: "Men of Israel [not just the Temple Elite], hear these words: Jesus of Nazareth . . . you crucified and killed by the hands of lawless men. . . . As your fathers did, so do you. Which of the prophets did not your fathers persecute? And they killed those who announced beforehand the coming of the Righteous One, whom you have now betrayed and murdered" (Acts 2:22, 23; 7:51, 52).

But, some might ask, "Why would they write this if it were not true?" Let us be reminded of the "Protocols of the Elders of Zion," a document alleging a conspiracy by Jewish leaders for world domination. This document has since been exposed as a blatant, anti-Semitic forgery, yet it still is being disseminated by Jew-haters. A lie is a lie, whether it is current or ancient; whether it has been reprinted in the millions of copies and believed by hundreds of millions as sacred Scripture. Truth is truth, even if it is believed by only a minority.

The aforementioned rabbi, who was debating on TV with the pastor, attempting to be magnanimous, remarked, "I have no quarrel with Christians or the New Testament." I too have no quarrel with sincere and good Christians. But I do have a quarrel with the New Testament. It is the root-cause of anti-Semitism. Christians are not going to deny, rewrite or censor the New Testament. It will forever be sacred to the Church. To the Church's credit, however, Christians are being admonished that the Jews are not to be held accountable for Jesus' death.

Mythology, when it embodies humanistic values, can be a worthy art-form. There are both good and bad mythologies. The "Passion of Christ," with its indictment of the Jewish People, is bad mythology. Its master plot is fairly summed up in the Christian doctrine of "Original Sin" – that the sin of our primal father is transmitted to the entire human race and redemption can come only by the sacrifice of a perfect human, namely, Jesus. John says Jesus was god-incarnate (John 1:1). The Jews, therefore, are regarded as "deicides" – killers of god. This is bad mythology, with no redeeming humanistic values. It would be unjust of God to hold the entire human race accountable for one man's sin. It would be cruel of God to sacrifice His son to save the human race – as though there were no other way for the omnipotent and merciful God to accomplish this. It is a preposterous and anti-humanistic notion that all non-believers are destined for eternal damnation. Moreover, Jesus' alleged sacrifice has not saved the world! Evil still exists. Bad mythology!

Gibson claims the movie is not anti-Semitic and protests that those who criticize it haven't seen the film. Read the *Book* and you will not have to see the film!

We must not be seduced into thinking this film is just an innocent art-form and will not feed anti-Semitism. While good Christians will not be incited to hatred of Jews, latent Jew-hatred surely will be awakened in the hearts of the psychologically impaired. The "sleeping dog" of anti-Semitism will be aroused by Gibson's masterful dramatization. This film is indeed hurtful to Jews. We can only hope for the day when enlightened Christians will recognize the New Testament as an anti-Jewish polemic, intended to exculpate Rome, vilify the Jews and legitimize Christianity.

The film's opening on February 25, 2004, will not be a felicitous day for Jews. It will be a serious set-back for the movement to humanize relations between Christians and Jews. Jews have endured enough of inquisitions, *auto-de-fe*, expulsions, pogroms and holocausts, without Gibson's reopening of the wound – without the twenty-first century cinematographic rendition of the crucifixion myth – without Gibson's attempt to re-legitimize the ancient canard of Jewish deicide. Surely, Jews and enlightened people everywhere are not advantaged by Gibson's attempt to express his own, narrow fundamentalism. Now, on the eve of Purim, we are pained by the appearance of this new, Hollywood version of the Christian myth. We can only pray, in the words of the *Shemoneh Esreh*, "For the slanderers, may there be no hope." The ancient lie is being dramatized as never before. Let us be informed and vigilant!

10

"Deicide"

Letter to *The Jewish World*

This is in response to Pastor Bill Adams' letter of March 4, 2004, in which he discusses Mel Gibson's movie, *The Passion*. Upon my first reading of the Pastor's letter, I was taken aback that a Jewish press should be a vehicle for purveying Christian doctrine. After reflection, however, I thought, *Gam zu l'tovah* – "This too is for the best" – because it allows for dialogue between Jews and Christians.

Pastor Adams states: "The insanity of the charge of 'deicide' still plagues us, as though someone could actually kill God." But let us be clear. Christian theology teaches that "god died on the cross." According to John 1:14, "In the beginning was the Word and the Word was with God and the word was god . . . and the Word became flesh and dwelt among us . . . ." (Cf. John. 12:45; 14:8-11; Philippians 2:6, 7; Colossians 1:15, 19; 2:9; Hebrews 1:3). Since Jesus is said to be the incarnation of God, those who allegedly called for his death are "deicides" – killers of God. Indeed, Pastor Adams acknowledges the "Incarnation" when he says Jesus was "a manifestation of God Himself."

The Pastor remarkably states: "Correct Christian understanding does not blame the Jewish people, but blesses them for bringing us everything most precious to us, including . . . *the atoning death of Jesus*" [Italics mine.]. Is Pastor Adams saying we Jews are responsible for the death of Jesus?

I am confused. I thought I heard Christian clerics try to exonerate the Jews by quoting Jesus' words, "No man takes my life from me. I lay it down of my own accord" (John 10:18)!

For the prophets of Israel, human sacrifice was abhorrent to God. God's rejection of Abraham's intended sacrifice of Isaac was an object-lesson, demonstrating God's repugnance of human sacrifice (Genesis 22). The Torah stipulates, "You shall not give any of your children to devote them by fire to Molech" (Leviticus 18:21; 20:2-5; Deuteronomy 12:31; 18:10; 2 Kings 3:26, 27). The first-born sons of Israel were redeemed by substitute animal-sacrifices as a protest against human sacrifice (Exodus 13:15). The prophets sought to move Israel away from sacrifice: "By loving-kindness and truth, sin is atoned for" (Proverbs 16:6). Hosea declared, "For loving-kindness have I desired and not sacrifice; and the knowledge of God more than burnt offering" (6:6). Cf. also Micah 6:6-8; Psalms 51:14-17; 40:6; 50:13,14,23; 69:30,31; 1 Samuel 15:22.

I am convinced Pastor Adams is a good person and loves the Jewish People. But his faith requires that he believe that only those who accept Jesus are worthy to be saved. One of the most oft-quoted passages of the Christian Scriptures is John 3:16: "For God so loved the world that He gave his only son, that whoever believes in him should not perish but have eternal life." This excludes Jews, Moslems, Hindus, atheists and all non-believers. God's so-called love of the world, therefore, is conditional and not universal. A logical paraphrase of John's saying would be, 'God so loved believers . . . .' In Judaism, what God requires is goodness, not the blood-sacrifice of a human. The prophet Micah declared: "He has showed you, O man, what is good and what the Lord requires of you but to do justly, love kindness and walk humbly with your God" (6:6-8).

Gibson's Passion movie does not bode well for Jews *or*

Christians. It promotes not love but anguish and confusion. The Gospel message of love is absent from Gibson's movie. I suppose Gibson believed violence would be a better seller. But there is one redeeming value. The Passion has engendered serious dialogue from which, hopefully, some good will flow.

11

Evangelical Support for Israel and
Missions to Jews

Letter to *The Jewish World*, February 22, 2004

I am responding to Pastor Bill Adams' letter of 1-9-04, commenting on my letter of 12-25-03, in which I addressed the pro-Israel stance of Evangelical Christianity and stated that the latter's position is predicated on the conversion *en masse* of Jews to Christ preceding his 'second coming,' and is a mechanism for such conversion. My original letter was in reaction to a solicitation from Chosen People Ministries, a missionary group dedicated to the conversion of Jews.

I accept Pastor Adams' assurance that many Christians support Israel out of pure motives. But let us be unequivocal about the official theology of Evangelical Christianity. The "Evangel" (Gospel, Good News) posits that 'Jesus died for our sins' and that 'salvation is only through him.' (John 3:16, 36). Thus, Jews and "non-believers" are eternally damned, and it behooves Christians to "save" them.

Pastor Adams states, "The Church is in the process of humbling herself and repenting of forced conversions and religious anti-Semitism . . . ." Of course Jews welcome this. But while forced conversions certainly are no longer countenanced, missions to Jews are alive and well. I quote from the letter from Chosen People Ministries: "The most important way we can bless the Jewish People is by enabling them to hear the good news that Jesus is the Messiah . . . . Chosen People Ministries missionaries . . . have prayed with hundreds of Jewish people to receive Jesus as their savior in Israel, Germany, the Ukraine, Canada, the United States and many other countries."

The regathering of the Jews to Israel as a precursor to Jesus' second coming is a fundamental belief of Evangelical Christians. The regathering is to be following by a mass conversion to Christ. The support of Israel by Christians, therefore, is a faith imperative.

I do not wish to impugn the motives of those sincere Christians who support Israel, Pastor Adams being among them. But I must ask Pastor Adams: Where does he stand on the pivotal Christian doctrine that "there is no other name [Jesus] under heaven given among men whereby we must be saved" (Acts 4:12); and that Jews who do not accept Christ are eternally damned? In contrast with this inhumane teaching, Judaism teaches that "the righteous Gentile has a share in the world to come" (Tosefta Sanhedrin xiii). The only true "bridge for peace" between Jews and Christians would be the repudiation of the doctrine of exclusive salvation and acknowledgement that goodness not creed determines one's standing with God.

Pastor Adams states Christian giving is motivated by the Abrahamic covenant, which promises blessings to those who bless Abraham's descendants – "I will bless those who bless you and curse those who curse you . . . and by you and your seed shall all the families of the earth be blessed" (Genesis 12:3; 22:18; 26:4; 28:14). Paul identifies the "seed" as Christ (Galatians 3:8). In Christian theology, the blessing proceeding from Abraham is through Jesus Christ. Christians bless the seed of Abraham by leading Jews to Christ. The Jewish interpretation of the Abrahamic promise is that the non-Jewish world is blessed by the Torah and Holy Scriptures, which originated with Abraham's Jewish descendants.

Christianity has, in effect, cursed the Jews by consigning them to eternal damnation. If Christians truly want to bless the descendants of Abraham, let them repudiate missions to Jews. Let them not seek to convert us. Let them respect our beliefs and recognize that we too are in the grace of God.

12

Jewish Survival—Jewish Pride

Isn't it curious—and somewhat depressing—that Jews are the only ones who seem to be concerned with survival, while Christian denominations such as the Pentecostals boast of vast increases in numbers? Jews, who have existed for millennia, should number in the billions—but their numbers are woefully small.

I thought about this at a recent synagogue service while observing a young man who was attending his classmate's Bar Mitzvah. The young man in question was wearing the latest street attire—long shirt, long, black silken knee shorts, the right sneakers, and a jewel embedded in his ear. On his head was the standard cloth synagogue kippah. Seated elsewhere was another young man, with a personal, knitted kippah, probably his own.

Observing these two young men, I thought about Jewish pride. What was the first young man proud of? I can't judge what was in his heart. But I did wonder, while observing the jewel embedded in his ear, whether the Torah was embedded in his heart. I also wondered what these two young men were thinking as they prepared to leave home for the synagogue. One probably checked his attire, making sure it conformed to the street culture. Was any thought given to the only outward sign of Jewishness—the kippah? The other boy made sure he had his own, special kippah. It also is interesting that the first boy sat during the Amidah and stood only when prompted by an adult. Both boys are Hebrew day school students.

Jewish survival is linked to Jewish pride. How do we create this? It is difficult. The usual Answer – and I think the correct one – is through family. Mom and Dad need to exemplify Jewish pride. Meaningful and heartfelt family rituals engender Jewish pride. But even given all these, we still need to be lucky and hopeful. Pop-culture is a powerful and irresistible influence, a tidal wave eroding Jewish pride. The young man with the ear stud may well develop into a fine, proud Jew. It is our fond hope he will.

Ours is a pluralistic society—sometimes called the "melting pot." Indeed, our Jewish identity is at risk of "melting" into the broader culture—becoming blurred, diffused. Unfortunately, many of our Jewish ancestors who immigrated to the United States were quick to cast off their Jewishness. Beards were discarded; family names were changed – "Goldstein" became "Gould." There are few outward symbols of Jewishness. The kippah discussed above is one. Another is calling each other by our Jewish names. We are taught the Israelite slaves in Egypt merited redemption because they did not change their Hebrew names. They did not attempt to camouflage their Jewishness by adopting the popular culture. Still another powerful agent for preserving Jewish identity is spoken Hebrew. If the aptitude for acquiring another language is lacking, the use of simple Hebrew phrases and greetings is an option.

When all is said and done, however, the surest formula for Jewish survival and Jewish pride is authentic Jewish knowledge. When we talk about Jewish survival we often think of fund-raising and edifices. These are necessities but learning – Torah study – is the way to Jewish pride and Jewish survival. *Talmud Torah k'neged kulam*—"The study of Torah supersedes all else." The Torah is an *Etz Hayim,* a "Tree of Life to those who take hold of it." A Jewish community whose priority is Torah-study is a strong Jewish community and will endure.

13
Judaism and Zen

I wrote the following to a Jewish professional — a good friend and committed Jew who practices meditation a la Zen Buddhism:

Pirke Avot teaches: "Who is wise? He who learns from everyone" (4:1). Through the ages, Judaism has not been inhospitable to appropriating the best of other cultures. But this must be done with sensitivity and diligence. Jews and Judaism are a fragile structure. The world historically has been inimical to Judaism Whereas, considering our ancient origins, we should number in the hundreds of millions or even the billions, our numbers are tragically few. As the saying goes, "It is hard to be a Jew." This is due not only to Jewish strictures but also to external pressures and allurements.

When the Israelites left Egypt, they constantly rebelled: "The people complained . . . and said, 'We remember the fish we ate in Egypt for nothing, the cucumbers, the melons, the leeks, the onions and the garlic but now our strength is dried up and there is nothing at all but this manna to look at'" (Numbers 11:1-5).

"Familiarity breeds contempt" — We Jews often grow weary of the familiar and hanker after what dazzles from without. This tendency is described in rather naked terms: "That you go not astray after your hearts and your eyes after which you go a whoring" (Numbers 15:39).

Judaism has meditation. It is called davening. The rabbis

were well aware of the human tendency to let the familiar and oft-repeated become perfunctory. They cautioned, "When you pray, let not your prayer become routine" (Pirke Avot 2:18). Meditation is not new to Judaism: "This book of the Torah shall not depart out of your mouth but you shall meditate therein day and night" (Joshua 1:8).

If there is something worthy in another culture, let us appropriate it. But let us do so with diligence and care, clothing it in Jewish garb, for ours is a fragile entity, continually under siege from within and without.

An individual was presented with a choice of two garments. The first was a new coat of fine fabric and splendid tailoring that fit perfectly. The other was old, worn, threadbare and ill-fitting. He chose the latter, saying, "This coat has been in our family for generations and is precious in my eyes. I shall repair it, preserve it and hand it down to my son."

To those tempted with the allurements of other cultures, the sage counsels, "Drink waters out of your own cistern" (Proverbs 5:15). With due diligence, whatever we seek we can find in the vast treasure that is Judaism. This writer learned this from personal experience.

14

A New Idolatry

A Shabbat sermon, Temple Israel, August 14, 1994

One of the great Hebrew bywords is *Shema!* – "Hear!" Hearing involves the auditory faculty but not necessarily the mind and heart. One may hear but *not listen*! To "listen" is to be attentive. Scripture uses the expression, "Incline your ear," which connotes deep interest and desire on the part of the listener. *Shema* epitomizes the essence of Judaism – a religion that values study: "If you have learned much Torah, do not congratulate yourself; for to this end were you created" (Pirke Avot 2:9). The Torah utilizes another word to motivate students: *Re'eh!* – "See!" This word begins the sidrah for this Shabbat. But what follows *re-eh!*, "See!" is not visual. No picture appears. In this instance, *Re'eh!* Implies apprehend, "See with your mind." Re'eh! alerts us to the high significance of what follows and urges our maximum attention.

The sidrah open with these words: "See, I have set before you this day blessing and curse. The blessing if you will heed the commandments of Adonai your God . . . the curse if you will not heed the commandments of Adonai your God but will go after other gods" (Deuteronomy 11:26-28). The temptation that beset the Israelites was base idolatry – the worship of gods of wood and stone. This, obviously, is not a temptation for Jews today – albeit, Jews do sometimes go astray after alien religions.

The present-day temptation is a different form of

idolatry – disguised idolatry, if you will. Let me here offer a different definition of idolatry, suggested by the following Psalm: "Their gods are silver and gold, the work of men's hands" (Psalms 115:4). "... the work of men's hands"! I am suggesting, therefore, that idolatry is essentially self-worship, extreme egotism – in a word – selfishness. If we are obsessed with self-aggrandizement – with our own goals and desires, with the acquisition of power, privilege, prestige and material things, to the exclusion of our obligation to others – this, indeed is a form of idolatry – of self-worship.

But we hasten to emphasize that Judaism does recognize that self-interest is a basic human drive. Judaism does not advocate asceticism. Consider the following prayer of reason: "Give me neither poverty nor riches; feed me with my allotted bread" (Proverbs 30:8). Poverty is not extolled nor is wealth denigrated. Moderation is the way of wisdom.

Pirke Avot teaches: "If I am not for myself, who will be for me? But if I am only for myself, what am I?" (1:14) – "What am I?" I am no better than a predatory animal. If we are to rise above the animal state, we must go beyond self-interest; beyond egotism. But that is not a simple task. Selfishness is innate whereas selflessness must be acquired with diligence, patience and good teaching.

We can learn about egotism from Cain, who slew his brother Abel. Cain was an egotist. When Cain's offering was rejected by God, Cain was distraught. God confronts him and asks: "Why are you downcast? If you do well, there will be uplift. If you do not do well, sin is couching at the door and its desire is for you." " There will be uplift"! You will rise above your basic animal nature. You will become fully human – to a status just below angels! God is admonishing Cain to go beyond himself – to combat the innate drive of selfishness which does not let us see beyond ourselves.

"You can rule over it." – We may not be able to subdue our selfish nature but we can control it. By 'doing well' – by controlling selfishness – Cain would be lifted up and rise above the predatory state and become eminently human.

"If you do well …" The mitzvot teach us how "to do well" – how to counteract selfishness. The mitzvot are commandments, not suggestions. Because of the power of our ego, we need strictures – commandments. But rather than binding or delimiting us, the mitzvot liberate and humanize us.

"See, I have set before you this day blessing and curse." We are free to choose. The Torah assists us in making the right choices. Kindness brings blessings – happiness, contentment and fulfillment. Selfishness brings the curse of sadness, pain and regrets.

The Torah is a Tree of Life which humanizes and frees us from the idolatry of gross egocentrism. The mitzvot bring blessings to our families, our friends and the world.

Later in the sidrah we read: "For you are a holy nation unto Adonai your God and Adonai has chosen you to be his most treasured people of all the nations of the world." This notion could have two opposing effects. Either it could make us haughty – chauvinistic – or it could make us humble, emulating the holiness of God who chose us to exemplify high morality to the world.

Today's sidrah behooves us to shun the idolatry of selfishness and admonishes us to keep the mitzvot, which humanize us and bring the blessing of peace.

Judaism, which is among the most humane religions known to mankind, is a religion of reason and love. Judaism recognizes our potential, grants us the freedom to choose how our lives shall be and guides us in the right choice. Let us thank God for the treasure of Judaism and Torah, the source of all blessings. Shabbat shalom!

15

The High-Way of Salvation
"A Night Vision"

I wish to speak of midnight experiences. The nighttime sometimes provides moments of lucidity and insight that surpass the intellectual activity of waking hours. Most night-dreams are fantasy, interpretable only by professionals, trained to penetrate the psyche. Occasionally, however, we may experience a night-dream which conforms to reality. It may be a reflection of our waking activities, thoughts and concerns, and may be potentially meaningful.

Recently, I awoke in the middle of the night with three compelling words: *HIGHWAY OF SALVATION*. At first blush, I had no idea what these words meant; but it was not long before they began to yield meaning. Coming as I did from an intense Christian experience in my youth, "Salvation" had been a prominent feature of my theology – one I fervently believed and preached. Since my return to Judaism, I had often given thought to the Christian concept of Salvation, vis-à-vis the Jewish concept. So, in the middle of the night, I stumbled out of bed, searching for a scrap of paper and a pen to record my thoughts – fragile thoughts which, in my semi-dreamlike state, would surely have slipped away like the early morning clouds before the rising sun. I will share with you those nighttime thoughts as I wrote them down and they took shape in the succeeding days. . . .

A highway is a public road – a route taken from one point to another. Thus, when we speak of *HIGHWAY OF SALVATION,* we need to ask, what is the starting point, the manner of travel and the destination? Or, we might resort to a fanciful definition for highway – a *high* way, that is, a *superior* way.

What do we mean by Salvation? What is Salvation in Christianity? What is the point of origin and destination on the Christian *HIGHWAY OF SALVATION?* The Apostle Paul writes: "By one man sin entered into the world and death by sin and so death has passed upon all men for that all have sinned" (Romans 5:12). Thus, the first man Adam sinned and transmitted sin and death to all his descendants. By "death" Paul means condemnation or total annihilation, with no hope of an afterlife. This is the point of origin on the Christian *HIGHWAY OF SALVATION.* As to the destination, Paul answers: "If because of one man's trespass death reigned. . . much more will those who receive the abundance of grace and the free gift of righteousness reign in life through the one man Jesus Christ" (Romans 5:17). The destination, then, on the Christian *HIGHWAY OF SALVATION,* is eternal life in heaven with Jesus. Jesus provides the only highway or road to heaven: "I am the way and the truth and the life. No one comes to the father but by me" (John 14:6). Regarding those who do not have Jesus, the Christian Scriptures answer: "He that believes not the son shall not see life" (John 3:16). Jews and "unbelievers," therefore, are excluded. This is not a *HIGHWAY* but a very *narrow* road!

What is the *HIGHWAY OF SALVATION* in Judaism – its point of origin, its destination and the manner of traversing it? In Judaism, man is not depraved or tainted with "original sin." Judaism teaches the soul we are given is pure and there is no irreversible transmission of sin-guilt to Adam's descendants.

Man was created at the conclusion of the creative week as the Creator's magnum opus. In what respect was man superior? He was a free moral agent, able to contemplate his own nature and praise his Creator. But with free moral agency comes struggle.

Man was endowed with a *yetzer tov* and a *yetzer ra* – a good inclination and an evil inclination. We see these two instincts playing out in the Cain and Abel drama in Eden. When Cain's offering was rejected by God, Cain was dejected. God said to him: "Why are you downcast? If you do well, there will be uplift. If not, sin is couching at the door and its desire is for you. But you can overcome it" (Genesis 4:6, 7). The two inclinations were at war with each other but Cain had the option to subdue his evil *yetzer*. Man is not irretrievably depraved but can rise above his baser instincts. This may require a lifetime of struggle; but to be human is to struggle. The Mishneh teaches: "Repent one day before your death" (Pirke Avot 2:10). Since we do not know the day of our death, we must struggle daily: "The path of the just is like the light of dawn which shines brighter and brighter until full day" (Proverbs 4:18).

We come into the world as humans. Judaism strives to make our basic human nature humane—benevolent, unselfish, concerned with the welfare of others. Yiddish calls a good person a *mensch*. Pirke Avot teaches: "Endeavor to be an *ish*" – a 'man' – humane (Pirke Avot 2:6).

How then does Judaism seek to traverse the highway of life? One needs a reliable roadmap. Guesswork and intuition are unreliable: "There is a way that seems right to a man, but its destination is the way of death" (Proverbs 14:12). For Jews the roadmap is *Halacha* – the Jewish Code of Law. *Halacha* is from the Hebrew root, to walk. Indeed, the patriarchs were said to "walk with God" (Genesis 6:9; 17:11). God admonished Solomon, "Walk in my statutes . . . and keep all my commandments" (I Kings 6:12). Judaism is called a "way of life."

It is written in the Psalms: "The Torah of Adonai is perfect, reviving the soul . . . . The commandment of Adonai is pure, enlightening the eyes . . . . By them is your servant warned and in keeping them there is great reward" (Psalms 19). When a Jew prepares to perform a mitzvah – a commandment – he thanks God for making us holy through His commandments.

As a play on the word "holy," the commandments make us "whole," or complete. They make us "wholly" human. They help to perfect us.

The rabbis cite three examples of obstacles on life's highway: "Three things remove one from the world: morning sleep [sloth, indolence] noonday wine, and frequenting the places of the ne'er-do-wells [the aimless, the irresponsible]." For "remove from the world," read — separate us from our higher humanity; from a life of purpose and service. Indeed, mitzvah entails responsibility

In the nineteenth psalm quoted above, we read: "Keep back your servant from presumptuous sins; let them not have dominion over me" (19:11). Let us call these, "sins of arrogance," where we put ourselves first, as Pirke Avot teaches, "If I am only for myself, what am I?" To be fully human is to balance personal concern with concern for others. The Psalmist continues: "In keeping of them there is great reward." This is not a material reward or a reward in the hereafter; it is the reward that comes from the joy of giving, of service. Indeed, service to others is the best therapy for depression and despair.

In Christianity, belief is paramount. In Judaism, deed is primary. The sage of Proverbs lists seven things God hates: "A proud look, a lying tongue, hands that shed innocent blood, a heart that devises wicked plans, feet that are swift to running to mischief, a false witness who speaks lies, and he who sows discord among brothers" (Proverbs 6:16-19). There is no mention of "unbelievers."

Christianity speaks of "being saved" (Ephesians 2:8), a single event in time. In Judaism, Salvation is a life-long process. The primary destination on Judaism's HIGHWAY of life is not the hereafter but rescue from a meaningless life — a life of selfishness, greed, hatefulness and aimlessness. Although Judaism does believe in the world to come, its main concern is the here and now: "The heavens, even the heavens, belong to Adonai, but the earth has He given to the children of men" (Psalms 115:16). Judaism teaches that we are "made in God's image" (Genesis 1:26, 27; 9:6) It is Judaism's purpose that we live up to our God-like nature. This requires a lifetime of striving.

In Christianity, Salvation is a supernatural act—one that is done *for* us (Ephesians 1:8). In Judaism it is something we do for *ourselves*: "Wash *yourselves*," declares the prophet Isaiah (Isaiah 1:16). God said to Cain: "You can overcome it" (Genesis 4:7). Judaism places the responsibility of character-development squarely on *our* shoulders.

Night-time experiences can sometimes prove meaningful. We have discussed the meaning of Salvation in Christianity and Judaism. The *HIGHWAY OF LIFE* has a point of origin, manner of travel, and destination. In Christianity, the sin of the primal parent infects the entire human race, resulting in perpetual death. The only remedy is belief in the sacrifice of Jesus. A moral life is of no avail. Non-believers are excluded.

As for the *HIGHWAY OF SALVATION* in Judaism and its point of origin, sin is not inherent and irreversible. God's plan was to create us imperfect so we might strive for perfection. We are created with a good and an evil inclination. It is given to us to overcome the evil inclination. Through the mitzvot, Judaism's moral imperatives, we endeavor to become more humane. Salvation in Christianity is a one-time event; in Judaism it is a process – to rescue us from our baser nature and elevate us to a higher, altruistic nature. This is Judaism's destination on life's highway – a *HIGH* way, a superior way – for the ennoblement of mankind. This was the lesson I learned in my night-time vision.

16

Atonement and Repentance

"AT–ONE–MENT"

In biblical times, atonement – forgiveness of sin – was done through sacrifice – a gift to the deity. Now it is through prayer, righteousness and repentance.

"Atonement" is *AT-ONE-MENT* – *at-one-ment* with ourselves, loved ones, friends, strangers and the planet. We are mind and body. Mind and body need to be at one – at peace – whole – in Hebrew *shalem*, akin to *shalom*. Anger, hate, selfishness, arrogance, sadness and ingratitude shatter the unity of body and mind, creating unhealth and stifling creativity and goodness.

We may be angry at ourselves – even hate ourselves. This destroys *at-one-ment*. We may be angry at others. This destroys *at-one-ment*. We may be selfish, withholding good from others. This destroys *at-one-ment*. We may be arrogant, diminishing the worth of others. This destroys *at-one-ment*. We may be ungrateful for goodness received and for life's blessings. This destroys *at-one-ment*.

At-one-ment is life's greatest challenge and greatest blessing. It is a perpetual struggle. Loved ones, friends and teachers may help our struggle but, ultimately, we alone can attain *at-one-ment*.

"Repent Every Day"

Apropos "The High Holy Days" – the period between Rosh Hashanah and Yom Kippur is called "The Ten Days of Repentance." While it is good to designate a specific period for repentance, there is a better way. Rabbi Eliezer taught: "Repent one day before your death" (Pirke Avot 2:15). When the disciples asked him, "Does, then, one know the day of his death?" he replied: "Let him, then, repent every day" (Avot de Rabbi Natan 15, 4). Taking daily inventory of short-comings is profitable for character-improvement. As for "holy" days – every day is holy, if only we would understand this. Rosh Hashanah – the Jewish New Year – is a celebration of Creation. This is good. But it is better to celebrate Creation *every* day.

17

Synagogue Issues

PAY TO PRAY

[*On February 3, 1968, I wrote the following to Rabbi Hayim Kieval:*]

As I entered the synagogue the evening of Yom Kippur, I could not help but notice the section in Founders Hall where college students were seated. I also overheard an usher tell a young lady she could not be seated in the main sanctuary but could sit in this area. From the response of the young lady, I sensed she felt deep hurt. The matter weighed on me and I found it hard to concentrate on prayer that night. Rabbi, you spoke that night of saving our youth for Judaism and recounted the soul-touching story of the great Rabbi Salanter who was late in coming to synagogue on Yom Kippur because he could not pray while a Jewish child was weeping. As I contemplated our fine young men and women and how little we honor them, I too could not pray. Our college students, in effect, are penalized for something beyond their control. Being students seems a liability. I wonder how many parents of college youth were sitting in synagogue during the High Holidays, concerned whether hospitality was being offered to their sons and daughters attending synagogue away from home.

Synagogues honor certain personages on the High

Holidays. These honors frequently are extended without regard to the degree of synagogue involvement. If we are sincere when we say the future of Judaism is with our youth, it is time we began to extend ourselves to them. "Who is honored? He who honors others" (Pirke Avot 4:1). In honoring our college youth, we demonstrate our confidence that the future of Judaism is theirs.

We need to entice our youth. The story is told of the teacher who had a fish pond. Whenever a child balked at coming to learn, he would entice him by letting him fish in his pond.

I propose setting aside a section of seats in the front of the main sanctuary—a place of honor as an earnest of our faith in our youth. It matters little whether these young men and women attend only once or twice a year. Some could become our most valuable assets in the future. Are there not a hundred Temple Israel members who would gladly forfeit their seats for these young collegians? I propose further that this special seating arrangement on the High Holidays be publicized on the college Hillel bulletin board.

When I was a young man, my uncle left Judaism. Among the reasons he cited was the practice of synagogues requiring tickets to pray on the High Holidays. I wonder how many Jews with a sense of decency have been lost to our people because of this irreligious practice. I know the response that if someone cannot pay, they need only make it known and there will be no problem. But this does not consider the embarrassment this would entail. A proud and sensitive person would simply forget the entire matter.

I have heard the familiar objection that we could not survive without the revenue of the ticket–incentive. But does this not show a lack of faith in the viability of our religion and in the Temple Israel family? If a financial short–fall should occur, I am certain our members would come forth.

We are taught a sin oft repeated takes on legitimacy. We

have become so accustomed to the practice of "tickets to pray" that we seldom hear any voices of protest. The first evening of Rosh Hashanah, as I looked out over our glorious sanctuary, I was overwhelmed by its splendor. When I beheld the vast multitude of worshipping Jews, I was reminded of the verse, "In the multitude of people is the king's honor" (Proverbs 14:28). Our sages have applied this passage to the glory that redounds to God when a large number of Jews are assembled for prayer. Our synagogue truly is a glorious institution. It has always been exemplary among American Jewish institutions. The hour is long overdue for Temple Israel to take the courageous, moral, religious and Jewish step and abolish ticket-requirements on the High Holidays. This would serve as an inspiration to synagogues across the nation. These days, egalitarianism is a passionate issue in synagogues. In matter of fact, the issue of ticket-taking is an egalitarian issue. Jewish law stipulates that a Jew is to be buried in a "plain pine box." This law was enacted to spare the poor shame and hardship. I believe this principle is operative regarding ticket-taking.

The old Beth Emeth synagogue on Lancaster Street had the following verse inscribed over its entrance: "My house shall be called a house of prayer for all people" (Isaiah 56:7). The black church housed there now has let this passage remain. What a noble thought! Why not make this a principle for Temple Israel? Have it imprinted on our stationary to become a theme as to what defines us.

God told the children of Israel: "Make Me a sanctuary that I may dwell among them" (Exodus 25:8). If our temple is to be considered a worthy sanctuary for God's presence, we must at last eliminate the ungodly and immoral practice of ticket-taking. Our renewed spirituality will generate a revival and draw spiritual-minded Jews into our midst.

The watchword of Temple Israel should be, "Let all your

deeds be done for the sake of heaven" (Pirke Avot 2:17). May we have the courage and vision to abide by this.

WOMEN IN THE SYNAGOGUE

The credo of Conservative Judaism is "Tradition and Change." A major change instituted by the Conservative Movement was the discontinuation of the long-standing practice of *Mechitsa* – seating women in the synagogue separate from men, often behind some barrier or in a balcony. The Conservative Movement also eliminated the morning blessing in which a male thanks God for not having made him a woman—a prayer many consider an affront to women. Formerly, this prayer was defended by traditionalists as not intended to demean women but to express gratitude for granting the male the mitzvot – mitzvot not binding upon the woman because of domestic obligations. Not withstanding, the Conservative movement opted to delete this prayer, substituting a prayer thanking God for creating us in His image.

Genesis 1:27 declares: "God created man in his image, in the image of God He created him; male and female He created them." At the expense of seeming facetious, we would suggest the latter statement was added editorially by a woman lest it seem only *man* was created in God's image.

In Orthodox synagogues, and some Conservative synagogues, women are not counted in a *minyan*—the required quorum of ten adults for Jewish congregational prayer. The Talmud warns of the seriousness of causing a woman to weep. I have been saddened at beholding the pained expressions on women when they were not counted in a minyan. The suggestion that 'men wont come if women are counted' is specious and not a legitimate reason to deny women their status. It is high time we discontinued this archaic, sexist and exclusionary practice.

At present, some Conservative synagogues still do not

grant women the privilege of being *ba-a-lot t'filah*—prayer leaders. We agonize over the loss of our children to Judaism. Teaching our young women to chant and lead congregational prayer surely would develop Jewish pride and commitment.

Historically, Judaism has been in the vanguard of exemplifying core human values. Sadly, however, in the matter of women's status in the synagogue, we are found wanting. As of January 29, 2009, President Barak Obama signed into law the Lilly Ledbetter Bill, granting women equal pay for equal work. It is long overdue that Jewish women were granted equal status with Jewish men. Justice has long been the cornerstone and bedrock of Judaism: "Justice, justice shall you pursue" (Deuteronomy 16:20). By taking a courageous stand on women's role in the synagogue, we may offend some. But the gain will far outweigh the loss, as we restore to our mothers, daughters, wives and sisters the dignity they justly deserve. They are precious in God's eyes and should enjoy all the synagogue privileges of their male counterparts.

"My house shall be called a house of prayer for all peoples"
(Isaiah 56:7)

Recycling Old Synagogue Buildings

Traveling abroad, one is struck by the many beautiful and wonderful old buildings. Preservation and restoration are part of the culture. By contrast, the tendency in this country has been to tear down and build anew. Fortunately, this is changing and preservation is taking hold.

With regard to synagogue buildings: The "throw–away" mentality often prevails. This syndrome is a reflection of our obsession with replacing perfectly good and serviceable possessions—kitchen cabinets, appliances, automobile and what have you.

If a synagogue structure is weakened beyond repair, structurally unsound or has outgrown the congregation, rebuilding might be an option. But there is something perverse and profligate about abandoning a beautiful and viable structure. The walls of our venerable synagogues have heard the prayers and joyful sounds of generations of Jews. This imparts a certain sanctity. In a time and in a culture of rootlessness, we need to preserve memory, linkage and a sense of permanence. Lack of pride is often a factor in our youth's indifference to their heritage and abandonment of Judaism. Preserving the old synagogue structures can help create pride of heritage.

This author's Bar Mitzvah was held in the old "Herkimer Street" synagogue, now occupied by a black church. One can only pass by the old synagogue and conjure up youthful memories. How wonderful it would have been if the Albany community had seen fit to preserve this venerable old synagogue!

Jews pray, "Renew our days as of old." Let us not hasten to abandon beautiful, old synagogue structures. Let us not be quick to "remove the ancient landmark."

As a postscript to the above, let us speak of environmental conservation. The Psalmist declares, "The earth has He given to the children of men" (Psalms 115:16). In the Garden of Eden, God charged Adam with the stewardship of the earth. Indeed, "Adam" is akin to the Hebrew *adamah,* 'earth.' Adam was an "earth-man." Preserving perfectly good Buildings – recycling them – is part of our obligation to be good stewards of our planet.

It is taught in the Talmud: Let not a man cast stones from his property onto public property. The story is told of a man who was removing stones from his property onto public property and someone discovered him. Scolding him, he said, "Empty-headed one! Why are you removing stones from property not yours onto property that is yours?" He laughed at him. Some time later he had to sell his field and was walking on that very same public property and stumbled on those very stones. He said: "Well did that man say to me: 'Why are you removing stones from property not yours to property which is yours'" (Baba Kama 50). This story relates to environmental conservation. When we defile and abuse the earth, we all are impacted.

In a similar vein, Rabbi Shimon ben Yohai taught: Some men were in a boat when one of them took a drill and began drilling under himself. His companions said to him: "Why are you doing this? He said to them: "Why do you care? Am I not drilling under my own seat?" They replied: "But the water is coming up and swamping the boat!" (Leviticus Rabah 4) Perhaps this story is the origin of the expression, "We are all in the same boat." Environmental conservation is a Jewish imperative. Preserving old synagogue buildings wherever possible is both a religious and environmental obligation.

"Remove not the ancient landmark" (Proverbs 22:28)

18

Thankfulness

A sermon, Shabbat Toldot, Temple Israel
November 25, 2006

Most of us have just experienced the pleasure of being with family and friends to celebrate the holiday of Thanksgiving. Through the years, there has been an ongoing debate whether Jews ought to celebrate Thanksgiving. In reality, Thanksgiving probably is the holiday most celebrated by Jews, after Passover and Hanukah.

The holiday of Thanksgiving may well have been inspired by the Jewish harvest festival of Sukkot. The concept of thanksgiving is a pervasive theme in Jewish prayer and holiday observance. On Shabbat we give thanks for creation; on Passover and Hanukah, for freedom; on Shavuot and Sukkot, for earth's bounty; and on Rosh Hashanah, for the New Year.

The Jewish prayer, the *beracha*, is the quintessential Jewish formula for expressing gratitude. When a Jew rises in the morning, he gives thanks for the new day, for sight, for clothing, for hope, for strength, for the earth, for the people Israel, for the Torah and for the provision of all our needs. In fact, it is meritorious to recite one hundred *Berachot* daily!

Life has positive and negative experiences. Obsessing on the negative induces sadness, despair, depression and, tragically, even suicide. Judaism encourages emphasizing the

80

positive by giving thanks for the good in our lives. Scripture counsels, "It is good to thanks" (Psalms 92:2).

Tradition tells that the first-century tanna, Nahum Gamzu, no matter how dire his circumstances, would say, *Gam zu l'tova,* "This too is for the best." His ills and disappointments never plunged him into despair. This attitude of optimism was already demonstrated by the Creator when he finally beheld His handiwork: "And God saw everything he had made and, behold, it was very good" (Genesis 1:31).

Another aspect of Jewish optimism is the hope of a future Messiah who will end violence and usher in everlasting peace. Isaiah prophesied, "The wolf shall dwell with the lamb and the leopard shall lie down with the kid . . . They shall not hurt or destroy in all my holy mountain....Nation shall not lift up sword against nation, neither shall they learn war any more . . ." (Isaiah 11:6—9; 2:4). Some might call this foolish optimism. We prefer to call it hopefulness. Hope encourages positive effort toward *Tikkun olam*—"Repairing the world." Despair brings resignation and surrender to evil.

When a loved one dies, a Jew recites the words, "Blessed is the righteous Judge." This is not to say death is in any way a blessing. Rather, it focuses on the blessedness of a life lost to us. In mentioning the deceased, we say, *Zichrono/ zichrona li-vracha,* "His/her memory is for a blessing." Instead of perpetually grieving over the loss of a loved one, we focus on how we were blessed by that one's life. The depressed focus inconsolably on the loss rather than the life, sinking into despair and inactivity.

Optimism and thankfulness are pervasive themes in Judaism. To be thankful and optimistic is to be emotionally healthy. Imitate the Creator and see the good and the beauty in the world. Resist evil but be not overcome by it. Be a "Nahum Gamzu" and seek redeeming elements in adversity. Hope for a better world and work toward it. Do not grieve excessively for loved ones but be blessed by their memory. Value each day and live life in a meaningful way.

19

"Who Is Rich?"

D'var Torah, Temple Israel Annual Meeting
June 24, 1980

Several weeks ago, at Shabbat minchah, there was a discussion on the mishnah in Pirke Avot – *Ezehu ashir? Hasemach b'chelko*—"Who is rich? He that is happy with his portion." This concept was criticized as discouraging progress.

But is the above admonition from Pirke Avot appropriate for our times or is it an anachronism? A recent article in "The New York Times" stated: "Economic recession, inflation and the rising rate of unemployment mean more than just having less money to spend. They are the components of a formula for personal and emotional turmoil, family tension and marital strife."

Indeed, poverty can be a calamity. Judaism does not extol poverty, as other religions sometimes have done, but takes a balanced view: "Give me neither poverty nor riches; feed me with the food that is needful for me" (Proverbs 30:8). Poverty is not the issue here but acquisitiveness. Our passion for progress has turned us into a generation obsessed with getting things – the latest brand, the newest model. Last year's wide tie, though worn only several times, is packed away for rummage. Unfortunately, this mania has even invaded our *shuls.* Perfectly good and serviceable furnishings are retired, to be replaced by the "latest styles." Thank God *Halacha* has preserved the Torah scroll from modernization.

What generates this mania for acquisitiveness? Is it an aspect of the *yetzer hara*? We want to *surpass* our fellow man. We hunger for adulation. But it is the wrong hunger – this passion to be praised for our material superiority.

Our concern should be otherwise: "Let not mercy and truth forsake you; bind them about your neck; write them upon the table of your heart. So shall you find favor and good understanding in the sight of God and man" (Proverbs 3:1-4). Our concern should be whether we have a *shem tov* – "a good name." Our *moral* status should be what concerns us. Even our synagogues have fallen prey to the current societal syndrome. We worry about our "image" – about the externals. The question we should be asking is, Are we a sanctuary of the spirit?

The wisdom of Pirke Avot – to be content with our portion – is still sorely needed, by individuals, families and synagogues. Proverbs counsels: "Better a dinner of greens and love therewith than a stalled ox and hatred therewith" (15:17). We can deal with less if there is love.

Balancing our fiscal budget is not the panacea for our ills. What *will* heal us is *emet* –'truth' and *chesed* – 'loving-kindness.'

20

Lashon Ha-ra –'Malicious Slander'
Sinat Hinam –'Gratuitous Hatred'

Of the seven things God hates (Proverbs 6:16—19), the last is "He that sows discord among brothers." This is done by setting brother against brother through character-assassination: "He that spreads strife is treacherous and a whisperer separates close friends" (Proverbs 16: 28). The motivation is *sinat hinam*–'gratuitous hatred.' *Lashon ha-ra* –'the evil tongue' – is a manifestation of *sinat hinam*. *Lashon ha-ra* is sometimes translated as 'malicious slander.' Slander implies untruth whereas *Lashon ha-ra* may be true or false. The intent is the key. Is it intended to elevate the speaker and denigrate the one spoken about? *Lashon ha-ra* may be motivated by jealousy. The speaker may have occupied a position of authority and had to relinquish his position to the one spoken against. There is rancor. The speaker, in effect, is saying: The one who replaced me is not worthy of my former position. *Lashon ha-ra* is insidious. One is convinced that because "it is true" – that the speaker is only trying to right a wrong – he is justified in spreading the information. But this is *sinat hinam*—'gratuitous hatred.' The accused is not present to defend himself. The one spoken to does not have all the facts. It is one-sided – the personal opinion of the speaker. If one has a cause against another, it is to *that* person one should go: "Debate your cause with your neighbor but reveal not the secret of another" (Proverbs

25:9, 10). If the matter concerns the community, there are procedures for dealing with this. Spreading malicious slander among individuals is not the way.

The Torah teaches: "You shall not go about as a talebearer among your people. You shall not stand idly by the blood of your brother" (Leviticus 19:16). The Hebrew word for "tale-bearer" is *rachil* – literally, 'peddler.' The slanderer's merchandise in trade is malicious tale-bearing. His 'going about' suggests tale-bearing is his customary practice. The rabbis teach the slanderer is worse than a murderer since he destroys the good name of the one slandered. This is underscored by the fact that the warning is followed immediately with, "You shall not stand idly by the blood of your brother." This also suggests listening passively to the slander – "standing idly by" – implicates the listener as an accessory to the sin, for slandering is ineffectual in the absence of a willing listener: "Where there is no wood, the fire goes out" (Proverbs 26:20).

Emphasizing the gravity of the sin of *sinat hinam*— gratuitous hatred – the Talmud asks: "Why was the first temple destroyed? Because of three things: idolatry, sexual immorality and bloodshed. But the second temple – when people were occupied with Torah, mitzvot and charity – why was it destroyed? Because of *sinat hinam* – 'gratuitous hatred.' To teach you that gratuitous hatred is equal to the three sins of idolatry, sexual immorality and bloodshed" (Talmud, Yoma 9b).

The above may sound like hyperbole. The point, however, is that sinat hinam, 'gratuitous hatred,' usually manifested by lashon ha-ra – 'malicious slander' – was regarded by the rabbis as a cardinal sin. The rabbis could not have appropriated a more graphic metaphor to illustrate their point than the destruction of the second temple. How is it possible that gratuitous hatred could be graver than idolatry, sexual depravity and murder? Because it is a common failing

– often occurring among, well-meaning, religious, prayerful and even scholarly individuals – for, indeed, it is for these primarily the teaching is intended.

Lashon Ha-ra – 'malicious slander' – is the most common manifestation of *sinat hinam* – 'gratuitous hatred.' We are taught that "it kills three: the speaker, the one spoken to and the one spoken about" (B. Talmud Arachin 15b). How is this "threefold" killing effected? If the slanderer is a community leader or authoritative figure, his authority and/or teaching are invalidated. The listener, who is a participant in the slander, is scandalized. The reputation of the one slandered is destroyed. The speaker may be a "religious" person, given to prayer. To such a one, God says: "Though you multiply prayer, I will not listen; your hands are full of blood" (Isaiah 1:11). Again underscoring the extreme gravity of this sin, we are taught, "He that engages in *lashon ha-ra* – 'malicious slander' – has no portion in the world to come" (Pirke de-Rabbi Eliezer 53).

21

"You Shall Not Stand Idly By . . ."

In our essay on *lashon ha-ra* – "malicious gossip" – we cited Leviticus 16:9: "You shall not go about as a tale-bearer among your people. You shall not stand idly by the blood of your brother." We interpreted this as willingly listening to gossip without protest – without admonishing the speaker, thus becoming complicit in the act: "Where there is no wood, the fire goes out" (Proverbs 26:20). Without a willing listener, gossip is ineffectual.

The question is how to react to malicious gossip? Should one refuse to listen to slander – in effect, turn a deaf ear? This would be the right course. A more difficult question is whether to admonish the speaker. As a rule, a *malshin* – slanderer – is arrogant and not amenable to reproof. Proverbs 9:8 says: "Reprove not a scorner lest he hate you. Reprove a wise man and he will love you."

R. Ilai said in the name of R. Eleazar son of R. Simeon: Just as it is commendable to say something that will be heeded, it is also commendable to refrain from saying something that will not be heeded (B. Talmud, Yevamot 65b). On the other hand we are taught: "You shall not hate your brother in your heart. You shall surely reprove your neighbor lest you incur sin on his behalf" (Leviticus 19:17). It is written: "The wise man – his eyes are in his head" (Ecclesiastes 2:14). A wise person will weigh whether the speaker is amenable to reproof. But the caveat of Rabbi Nathan is sobering: "Reprove not your neighbor for a blemish that is yours" (Baba Metzia 59b). We are cautioned, "Be not wise in your own eyes . . . be not righteous overmuch" (Proverbs 3:7; Ecclesiastes 7:16).

In any event, we must be careful not to be complicit in slander but tactfully decline to listen. Resh Lakish taught: Reproof leads to peace . . . "All peace that has no reproof with it is not peace" (Genesis Rabah 54:3).

22

Love and the Healing Tongue

"Remove not the ancient landmark" (Proverbs 22:28) – We have used this quote earlier as applying to the inclination to discard venerable old synagogue buildings and replace them with new, often sterile, modern structures. Utilizing poetic license, we are now applying the above passage differently. These "ancient landmarks" are old formulas for human relationships we have heard over and over again until they seem to become clichés. Because of their oldness and familiarity, we tend to take them for granted. But these "old landmarks" still have much to teach us. Each one is challenged to find his own meaning.

LOVE

The sage of Ecclesiastes taught: "Two are better than one for they have a good reward . . ." (4: 9). One without another may gain happiness and have a meaningful life. But two, together, can be happier, more creative and live more meaningfully. This, counsels the sage, is the optimal human experience. The union of two – male and female – conforms most closely to nature's way and intention. But for this union to be happy and creative there must be love.

"Love covers a multitude of sins" (Proverbs 10: 12). Love understands that to be human is to be fallible. Love is challenged and activated when confronted by imperfection. Thus, "Two are better than one" – if love defines the relationship. Two are not better than one where there is enmity. Love, in the above context, embodies mutual respect, acceptance of differences, acknowledgement of imperfectness and compassion for foibles and failures. Love is limitless and constant. This kind of love is the highest human achievement. It is a remedy for depression and formula for creativity.

One of the most fortuitous human events is the union of a man and a woman whose love is unequivocal, from the outset and until the end. It fulfills a great human need, for "It is not good that man [and woman] should be alone" (Genesis 2: 18). This is our nature; this is how we were created.

Whereas "love" is generic, "unselfishness" is definitive. We paraphrase Pirke Avot, 'Let the being of the other be as dear to you as your own.' One who is emotionally healthy will rightfully think well of himself. That self-esteem will translate to esteem for the other. This is our definition of unselfishness. This is the meaning of "Love the other as you do yourself" (Leviticus 19: 18). Though we hear this admonition often, it should never become a cliché. It should be fixed in our hearts and be as constant as the stars in the heavens. It is a path to ultimate happiness and full humanness.

"A Time to be Quiet and a Time to Speak" (Ecclesiastes 3: 7)

How we use speech is an essential component in human relationships – especially in marriage. "Death and life are in the power of the tongue" (Proverbs 18: 21). To emphasize the potential, destructive power of the tongue, the sage mentions "death" first.

While the tongue can do great damage, it has great healing power: "A soothing tongue is a tree of life ...There is that speaks like the piercings of a sword; but the tongue of the wise is healing ... Pleasant words are as a honeycomb, sweet to the soul and health to the bones" (Proverbs 15:4; 12: 18; 16: 24). The sage commends tactfulness: "The heart of the righteous studies to answer" (15:28). To use an old adage – a person of tact "thinks before he speaks." A wise and sensitive person knows the right word and the right time for speaking: "A word fitly spoken is like apples of gold in settings of silver" (25: 11).

"WHO IS MIGHTY? HE WHO CONTROLS HIS INCLINATION" (PIRKE AVOT 4: 1)

How we deal with our own anger and that of others is another important component in human relationships. Some behaviorists have advised "getting it all out." The sages, however, advise restraint: "He that is slow to anger is better than the mighty; and he that rules his spirit than he that takes a city" (Proverbs 16: 32). To respond with anger to an angry person is only to increase strife: "The beginning of strife is when one lets out water; therefore leave off contention before the quarrel breaks out" (Proverbs 17:14). Being human, there are times when we will be angry. What we do with that anger is critical. If we let it burst forth, the consequences may be dire: "Anger rests in the bosom of fools" (Ecclesiastes 7:9). The plain meaning is – not to get angry. But if you can not avoid becoming angry, let it not consume you; let it not fester; let it pass lest you act imprudently.

How shall we deal with an angry person? "A soft answer turns away anger" (Proverbs 15:1). Or, one may choose not to react: "A fool speaks all his mind but a wise man keeps it back and stills it" (Proverbs 29:11). This may be the better choice when dealing with one who is irrational or emotionally disturbed. Sometimes the emotions between husbands and wives and between parents and children are so charged and passionate that the best response is no response. A wise person knows when to speak and when to refrain from speaking.

PRAISE/FLATTERY

Above, we cited Proverbs 18:21: "Death and life are in the power of the tongue," demonstrating the healing and/or destructive capability of the tongue. Speech comes into play upon our first encounter with another person. To greet a person with *shalom* is healing. It is told of Rabban Yohanan Ben Zachai, "No one ever preceded him with [the greeting of] shalom – even the non-Jew in the marketplace" (Talmud Berachot 17; cf. Pirke Avot 4:20). We are taught: "Receive everyone with a cheerful countenance." No, this is not from Dale Carnegie. It is the 2000-year old teaching of the Tanna Shammai (Pirke Avot 1:15). Dale Carnegie in his book does say: "Be hearty in your approbation and lavish in your praise" (*How to Win Friends and Influence People.*) Indeed, praise is a Jewish virtue: "Praise is fitting for the upright" (Psalms 33:1; cf. 92:2). If it is fitting to praise the Creator, how much more so is it to praise His creatures (Cf. Gen. 9:6).

What is the nature of praise? Praise is the verbal recognition of the worth or merit of another. True praise is heart-felt. It seeks no advantage for itself. It is a giving, not a receiving. Its purpose is to heal, to encourage and to bless. We are taught, "Judge every one in the scale of merit" (Pirke Avot 1:6) – Seek out the virtues in others; magnify and acknowledge them.

Praise and flattery are not the same. Flattery seeks personal advantage. It is not heart-felt but opportunistic. "To flatter is to steal" (Yiddish proverb). Hebrew speaks of *g'nevat daat* – "stealing the mind" – deception. The flatterer poses as a friend and admirer but his purpose is to manipulate. He is self-seeking. Flattery is a "verbal bribe" (Abraham Bloch, *Book of Jewish Ethical Concepts*). A flatterer speaks with a "double heart" (Psalms 12:3). "A flatterer's lips and heart are not one" (Talmud Pesachim 113b).

The sum of the matter is regard for the worth and dignity of our fellow human beings. We demonstrate our attitude by word, by deed and – even by silence. Yes, merely by listening with sincerity and intention to the speech of another is an act of loving kindness. We speak of "alternative healing" – of herbal and non-medical remedies. The healing tongue should be added to the roster of alternative healing strategies. The tongue has the power to heal. It is within our power to so use it.

23

The "Thirty-Six Righteous"

Legend has it that in every generation there are thirty-six righteous for whose sake the world endures. In Hebrew they are the "*Lamed-Vav Tzadikim* or "Lamed-Vavniks." They are found throughout the world and in every sphere of life. They are ordinary trades people and are not distinguished by great learning but by goodness and humility. They are unknown to each other and would deign proclaim themselves to be of the "Thirty-Six Righteous."

The following lessons may be drawn from the legend of the *Lamed-Vavniks*:

1. A humble person of no particular learning or status need not feel insignificant or inferior before the mighty and the great. Only an upright heart and good deeds merit being of the Thirty-Six Righteous.
2. The mighty and the great should neither demean the simple nor reserve their esteem for the rich and powerful.
3. "The righteous are the foundation of the world." – The ultimate criterion of human worth and usefulness is not power and wealth but righteousness.

4.   The legend of the Thirty-Six Righteous affirms the dignity of man and is a great equalizer.

24

"Which Is the Right Way?"
(Pirke Avot 2:1)

It is the nature of religious teachers to seek concise definitions that reflect the essence of religion. In addressing Judaism, we are confronted with a complex and ancient civilization, with a vast compendium of theological and ethical literature – the creation of prophet, priest, sage, legalist and moralist. Many have endeavored to arrive at definitions that embody the totality of Judaism. Below are some examples, both ancient and modern:

The prophet Micah represents one of the early attempts at summarizing the *right way*: "He has showed you, O man what is good and what Adonai requires of you but to do justice, love kindness, and walk humbly with your God" (6:8).

Simeon the Just taught: "The world stands upon three things: On the Torah, on divine service and on acts of loving kindness" (Pirke Avot 1:2).

The above examples share two elements. They favor the number three and consider loving-kindness a core value.

The late Rabbi Imanuel Rackman referred to Judaism as "God-centered humanism" – a term which reflects Genesis 9:6: "Whoever sheds man's blood, by man shall his blood be shed; for God made man in His image." Humanism is reverence for human life. "God-centered humanism" is based on the premise that because man is created in God's image, he has infinite worth. Below are other approaches to defining the essence of Judaism:

A gentile came to Shammai and said: "Convert me – but on condition that you teach me the whole Torah while I stand on one foot." Shammai dismissed the man summarily. The gentile went to Hillel who accepted him for conversion. Hillel said, "That which is hateful to you, do not unto your fellow man. This is the whole Torah. The rest is commentary. Go forth and learn" (Talmud, Shabbat 31).

What does the above tale teach us? – *Mah zeh ba l'lamdenu?* A true teacher seeks for the essence of things – especially how they impact our lives. The gentile's intention was not to seek knowledge but to confound and/or antagonize the rabbi. Shammai had no patience for the man and thrust him out. The gentile came to Hillel with the same intent but Hillel, instead of rebuffing him, judged him "in the scale of merit." He gave him the benefit of the doubt and accepted him for conversion. A passage from Proverbs comes to mind: "If your enemy is hungry, give him bread to eat. And if he is thirsty, give him water to drink; for you will heap coals of fire upon his head" (Proverbs 25:22). The gentile came as an adversary, with hostile intent; Hillel gave him 'bread to eat and water to drink, heaping coals of fire upon his head.' He turned hostility into desire, disarming his would-be adversary. Hillel followed the example of Aaron: "Be of the disciples of Aaron, loving peace and pursuing peace, loving mankind and drawing them close to the Torah" (Pirke Avot 1:12). It is written, "One should always be gentle as Hillel not irascible as Shammai" (Shabbat, 30b).

Hillel's approach was exemplary. It demonstrated his ability to judge the capacity and disposition of his client and not overwhelm him. It also is an object lesson for teachers to give students concise definitions which they can remember and carry as a standard. Finally, it teaches us a core value of Judaism.

Rabbi Akivah taught the great principle of the Torah is, "Love your neighbor as yourself" (Leviticus 19:8). Rabbi Judah ha Nasi said: "What is the right way one should choose for himself? That which is an honor to him and brings him honor from his fellow man" (Pirke Avot 2:1). This teaching reflects the balance Judaism tries to achieve between self-preservation and altruism. This balance is also represented in the teaching of Hillel: "If I am not for myself, who will be for me. But if I am only for myself, what am I" (Pirke Avot 1:14). Of these two, the second is the more challenging. Self-preservation is instinctive; unselfishness is less so. To inculcate the virtue of altruism, we need good role-models and good teaching.

"Rabbi Simeon said: There are three crowns: the crown of Torah, the crown of priesthood and the crown of kingship. But the crown of a good name excels them all" (Pirke Avot 4:17). How is this so? Sadly, there are impious men even among Torah scholars. This is the thrust of Rabbi Hanina ben Dosa's Dictum: "He whose wisdom exceeds his deeds, his wisdom is invalid" (Pirke Avot 3:12). Priesthood is a matter of inheritance. Kingship is dynastic. According to Rabbi Simeon, acquiring and maintaining a good name by living virtuously and unselfishly is the most meritorious of the four crowns, for it brings peace and harmony into the world.

Distilling the vast compendium of Jewish knowledge into concise definitions aids our understanding and lends direction. It is like the ancient mariner navigating his vessel by the North Star to bring him safely to his destination. Or the rope of the mountain-climber which enables him to reach the pinnacle of the mountain. Or the single match which ignites a fire. Love of fellow-man is the bright North Star of Judaism. The rest of Jewish learning is a vast galaxy requiring a lifetime of learning.

If this planet with its teeming millions is to survive, we must learn how to dwell together in mutual respect and peace. This is the essence of Judaism. This is *the right way one should choose.*

25

Arrogance Blinds Us to the
Good in Others

Judaism is *this-life* centered. The precepts of Judaism are intended to enhance life. Respect for others is a core-value of Judaism.

The story is told of Rabbi Eleazar, the son of Rabbi Shimon, who was coming from his teacher's house in Migdal Eder. He was riding on a donkey along the river, rejoicing greatly and feeling elated at having learned much Torah. He encountered a man who was exceedingly ugly. When the man greeted the rabbi, the rabbi did not return the greeting but said to the man, "Imbecile— how ugly you are! Are all the people of your city as ugly as you?" The man replied, "I do not know. But go and tell the Craftsman who made me: 'How ugly is this vessel you have made!'" When Rabbi Eleazar realized he had sinned, he dismounted his donkey, prostrated himself before the man and said: "I beg of you, forgive me." The man replied: "I shall not forgive you until you go to the Craftsman who made me and say to him, "How ugly is this vessel you have made!" Rabbi Eleazar followed the man until he reached the city. The people of the city came out to greet the rabbi and said to him: "Peace be unto you, our master, our master, our teacher, our teacher." The man said to them: "Who are you calling, 'our master, our master?'" They said to him, "The one who is walking behind you." He said to them, "If this one is a rabbi, may the likes of him not increase in Israel!" They said to him, "Why?" He said to them, "Thus and thus he did to me." They said to him, "Nevertheless, forgive him, for he is a great teacher of Torah." He said to them, "For your sake I shall forgive him — only let him not continue this practice" (Taanit 20).

The above story is an example of arrogant and unseemly behavior by a scholar. The following sayings from Pirke Avot apply:

"Do not despise any person" (4:3).

"Let the honor of your fellow man be as dear to you as your own" (2:15).

"Who is deserving of honor? One who honors others" (4:1).

At the head of the list of the seven things God hates is arrogance — *enayim ramot*— "haughty eyes" (Proverbs 6:16-19). This is a remarkable insight [no pun intend] into the dynamic of arrogance. It concerns how we *see* others. "Haughty eyes" suggests when we look *at* others, we do not look at them but *over* them. We *overlook* them. We see them in a negative light. We do not apprehend who they really are but discount them. We are so filled with ourselves we cannot make room for another. Pirke Avot teaches, "Judge everyone in the scale of merit" (1:6) — with the scale weighted in their favor, giving them the benefit of the doubt; endeavoring to see their merit. But arrogance blinds us to the good in others.

There is a wonderful balance in Judaism. For example, "If I am not for myself, who will be for me? But if I am only for myself, what am I" (P. A. 14). While we are taught arrogance is to be eschewed, this is not to say we should be self-deprecating. Indeed, we are taught, "Be not evil in your own eyes" (P. A. 2:18). Rabbi Simcha Bunem of Przysucha taught: Every person should have two pockets. In one pocket there should be a piece of paper saying, "I am but dust and ashes." When one is feeling excessively proud, he should reach into this pocket, take out this paper and read it. In the other pocket there should be a piece of paper saying: "For my sake the world was created." When one is feeling disconsolate and lowly, one should reach into this pocket and take out this paper and read it. We are each the joining of two worlds. We are fashioned from clay but our spirit is the breath of Adonai (*Tales of the Hasidim Later Masters*, Martin Buber, pp. 249—250).

The sage of Proverbs taught: "Let a stranger praise you and not your own lips" (27:2). At first blush, this may seem like arrogance – seeking the praise of others. Rather, one should not be uncomfortable about being acknowledged for worthy deeds.

"Most men will proclaim every one his goodness but a faithful man, who can find?" (Proverbs 20:6). This is sometimes interpreted as: Many make promises but few carry them out. I would suggest another interpretation: Boastfulness is common but genuineness is rare.

"He who pursues honor, honor flees from him" (Rabbinic saying). Such a one may achieve high station but not receive honor. This is because the purser sought power for power's sake, not for service. This is similar to, "A name made great is a name destroyed (P.A. 1:17). Because this person's motive is the pursuit of honor and power, he is ultimately recognized for what he is and repudiated. "It is better to be told, 'go up, go up,' rather than, 'go down, go down'" (Leviticus Rabah 1:5). In the company of the wise, integrity is honored; mediocrity and insincerity are not.

Arrogance is an overweening opinion of one's worth, coupled with a diminished opinion of the worth of others. Pride is an honest appraisal of one's worth, coupled with respect for others. This kind of pride is salutary.

26

Insights

SELFLESSNESS

Is there any giving that is pure – when the "self" gives up something without hope of gain? When I visit the sick, is it because my religion tells me to? Because the recipient will think highly of me? Because it makes me feel proud? If my motive is not pure, does it matter so long as the sick are comforted and their spirits lifted? If we were to obsess on our human imperfectness, ever pondering our lack of pure motives, would we ever give? We need to be comfortable with our "humanness" and take the "leap of faith" – not reflecting too much on motives but doing the loving act. Judaism teaches, "Be not evil in your own eyes" (Pirke Avot 218). Be *impressed* not depressed with your self.

It has been said the only pure love is parental love. But even this may not be wholly pure because the child is the only entity wholly from me. Therefore my love and my forbearance are essentially for and toward myself. But, if the child is helped, renewed, and affirmed, the love-act is worthy. This is good because it is human nature playing out.

How shall we *receive* selflessness? By graciously accepting selflessness, we affirm the other. In fully accepting, we fully give—"repay" the selflessness. It is good also to repay in a tangible way. Humans need to reciprocate. It is an essential human exercise. It is not tainted. It is our nature playing out.

"Teach Us to Number Our Days" (Psalms 90:12)

Mark the transitoriness of life so each day is cherished and our time is filled with all possible meaningfulness. Most live their lives, following whatever the day brings. Others live intentionally, initiating activities of meaning.

"As We Sow . . .

Heaven and hell are not places apart from us. They are in our heart. As we sow, so shall we reap. If we sow seeds of love and truth, we shall reap almonds and roses. If we sow seeds of lying and hate, we shall reap thistles and thorns. But it is not given to all to plant rightly. Heaven weeps over two: Those who do not know to sow rightly and those who know and do not sow rightly.

The preacher taught: "Whatever your hand finds to do, do it with your might . . . (Ecclesiastes 9:10).

Encounters

Webster defines "encounter" as a 'meeting with hostile intent.' We have daily encounters which often reflect our primeval, predatory instincts to view strangers with suspicion. But if we yield to our yetzer tov – our "good instinct" – we may be rewarded with the discovery that the "faceless" one indeed has a divine face. I experienced a poignant example of this: A member of our congregation who was president during my tenor as cantor had made life difficult for me. He seemed like a "non-person." Recently he approached me to commend my chanting of the Haftorah. I looked intently into his eyes and beheld the "divine image." It was as though I had rediscovered him. How many missed opportunities we daily have. Thus, it is ours, either to cheat ourselves of warm human meetings, or bless ourselves.

"A Time to Love"

"There is a time for everything under the sun . . . a time to love . . ." (Ecclesiastes, ch. 3). Why do head and heart ache? Because we keep the portals of love closed. We cannot shackle the spirit without suffering harm. Only by loving and being loved can we fully open the portals of the heart. This is the elixir for a wounded and suffering soul.

"Because I Make Them Happen"

I have always thought "outside the box." As a youngster, I dragged orange crates home for the corner grocery and constructed bird houses with the crudest of tools. When my contemporaries were partying and going to the movies, I was off on my bicycle with my best friend – hiking, camping and bird-watching. I always followed my heart. My path had risks but also potential rewards. When I taught, I would bring my students stories of my real-life experiences and invariably they would ask, "Mr. Picker, how is it so many things happen to you?" My response would be, "Because I *make* them happen." Most of us walk through life carefully, on solid ground, one step in front of the other. I, for my part, run and leap, my spirit soaring and taking wings. My life has not been trivial. I have always been breathless and impatient to experience, to embrace. I suppose this is what differentiates the poet from the pragmatist. Great expectations can result in great disappointments. On the other hand, they can have great rewards. This is the lot of the poet and the dreamer.

"It is Not Good for Man . . ."

"God said, 'It is not good for man to be alone. I will make him a fitting helper'" (Genesis 2:18). This makes God out to be compassionate and caring. But it also puts woman in a lesser light. She is a "helper" – subordinate; essentially a servant. The woman is fashioned from man's body; she derives from him and is a piece of him – his possession, as it were. The rabbis ameliorate this in the Midrash: "From his side" – to be at his side, to aid and cherish him. By the same token, the man is to cherish his wife as his own flesh.

But a better understanding of marriage is the first creation account, "Male and female He created them." They were created together as equal partners. In that case, it would have been better to say of the woman, 'It is not good that she should be alone. I will find her a fitting partner.' The rabbis have a saying which riles women: "Go up a step and choose a friend. Go down a step and choose a wife" On the other hand, the Talmud states: "A man should always be careful about wronging his wife. Since her tears come quickly, punishment for wronging her is quick to come" (Baba Metzia 59a).

INSPIRATION

"Inspiration" literally is 'breathing in.' It is not an ordinary breath but a deep breath that fills every crevice of the lungs. It is a moment that was not present before – a spontaneous moment, an awakening, and a stirring. Many experience moments of inspiration but not many are able to develop these seed-moments into greater, meaningful structures. Poets, writers and scholars do. They *secure* the inspirational moment and make it grow. Like a tree that develops annual growth-rings, the scholar builds upon learned experiences and increases knowledge. How sad are they who never grow;

who are the same yesterday, today and tomorrow. How fortunate are they whose "light shines brighter and brighter until the perfect day." For the creative, the new day is a time of opportunity and renewed growth. For others, it is a wondering how to pass the day.

WHO THINK IN ABSOLUTES

There are those who think in absolutes. What differentiates the dogmatist from the reasonable person? The former makes an assertion but never follows it with "therefore." The reasonable person asks, with our sages, "What do we learn from this?" What are the implications, consequences and right response?

A DIFFERENT "I AND THOU"

Because of a delightfully warm, spring day, many came to walk the trails at Five Rivers. But I wondered how many were in the elemental mode of just enjoying the sensual pleasure of that perfect afternoon. The elemental mode and nothing more. I thought of Buber's "I and Thou" as applicable to another plane of "intentional" interaction; as applied to our connection with nature. By truly knowing the flora and fauna, nature is no longer an "it" but a "thou."

This linkage humanizes us because we are essentially Adam – earth – and must maintain our innate connection with our source and its hosts. Thus, when we traverse nature, we walk on a much higher plane.

VOICES

We have spoken of being in "touch" with mother-earth. Withdrawing from mall and automobile and touching our feet to pure ground – our matrix mother-earth. We need also to withdraw betimes from the cacophonous jangle of technology, the intrusive drone of the highway, the ubiquitous ring-tone of the cell phone, the squeaks and squeals of the computer, the harsh sounds of video and pop-music. To withdraw and repair to mother-earth's voice and the voices of her wild children – the wind singing in the trees, the frogs croaking in the wetlands, the birds caroling in the trees and fields, the buzzing of insects, the gentle tinkle of the mountain brook on the stream-bed's stones . . . . We are a noise-generating civilization that needs to pause and quietly stand and listen to the voices of mother-earth. We need to do this for our self-definition and to rediscover our own, true nature.

BLESSED RAIN

Gentle rains have been falling. The parched ground and vegetation are singing again!

TO SCALE THE PEAKS

Life is a landscape of planes, hills, valleys and peaks. It is a blessing when we can scale the lofty peaks.

SHEHECHEYANU

The animal instinct is to survive – to forage, to prey, to take. The spiritual person is thankful for being a recipient. The animal looks forward or downward, ever seeking to satisfy its needs. The spiritual person looks beyond and upward – transcending and ever acknowledging what has been received.

Judaism recites the *shehecheyanu* prayer on special, joyous occasions. It is a prayer of thanks for having lived to enjoy that special moment. I propose we recite it daily, yes hourly, even every minute. If not recited, at least thought. When we open our eyes to new life each morning, say *shehecheyanu* for sight and the new day. When we take an exhilarating breath of air, say *shehecheyanu* for air and the ability to breathe.

Say it when we smell a new fragrance; when we meet

a cherished friend; when we taste a fruit or morsel of food. The list is as endless as life's gifts. Thus the spiritual person is in a constant state of thanksgiving. The spiritual person is a *shehecheyanu* person. This is the true antidote for depression and melancholy. We need not forage for this gift anywhere else but in our own field of Judaism. Say *shehecheyanu* for our Jewish heritage which teaches us how to attain true spirituality!

ALIYAH – GOING UP

We begin life at ground zero – our basic animal nature. Our progress through life should be a constant aliyah – an ever "going up" – from basic animal nature to a higher spiritual plane. What elevates, what ennobles, what leads to the higher spiritual plan is the Torah. Moses had to ascend on high to receive the Torah. Each Jew must make his own ascent to Sinai: "The path of the just is as the shining light which shines brighter and brighter until day's zenith" (Proverbs 4:18). Only a life of ever "going up" is a worthy life.

"PURIFY OUR HEARTS . . ."

The Shabbat prayer says, "Purify our hearts to serve you in truth." Our service to God will only be true when it is our own, not something superimposed which we duplicate unquestioningly and meaninglessly. Only when we have searched and found does our Judaism become vital and transforming.

Healthy Regression

There are times when one needs to regress to childhood; to renew the luster of life and experience wonder, dazzle, glee and spirit-uplift. On a pristine, sunny morning, we had set out for bird-watching. It was the migratory season for transient birds, the most sought-after being the warblers. On our previous walks, we had been hearing a warbler but were uncertain of its identity. Its song was a thin zee ,zee ,zee, zee, zee, zee, zee, ascending upward. We were eager to spot our quarry for a positive identification. We walked up the road past the railroad tracks and descended down a path among small trees and shrubs, jumping across a small stream and ascending the next hill. We could hear our *zee, zee, zee* bird but it kept eluding us. After about an hour of following the song, we spotted it briefly but not long enough to identify it. Constantly changing our position and moving through the brush, our patience finally was rewarded and our bird came into view. We could hardly contain our excitement. Yes, it was what my friend had suggested – a Prairie Warbler – mostly yellow, with two black face marks and broken black stripes down the sides. We congratulated each other and felt child-like wonder, dazzle, glee and spirit-uplift. It was a moment of regression to childhood for which we felt privileged and thankful. A tiny, feathered mite was able momentarily to transform two staid adults into gleeful children – a healthy regression. We were captives of the magic that is bird-watching.

"The Children of Angels"

The other day at Five Rivers, my favorite haunt, I had a tender encounter. A tiny blue butterfly was fluttering in my path and I thought it might be a Karner Blue – a not too common species seen primarily in our locale. Gently, slowly, quietly, I bent down for a closer look. To my gratification, it did not start. I took a twig and carefully placed it next to the butterfly, hoping it would light upon it. It did. I lifted it aloft to peer more closely and could discern the tiny spots on its underside. It stayed on the twig as though it sensed no danger from me and I felt a spiritual connection with it.

If birds are, as I imagine, our angels, then butterflies are the children of angels. We speak of "bird-watching" – why not "butterfly-watching"? Birds help our spirits soar; butterflies do so too. We need to free our spirits from darkness, decadence, unkindness and insensitivity and bathe them in nature's pristine purity.

Privileged Moment

When I was a lad in Scout camp in the late thirties and a novice bird-watcher, I experienced a "privileged moment" that has never departed my memory. The common chickadee, which then was new to me, had chanced to frolic in a White Pine only a few feet from me and I was able to observe it for quite some time. I was in a state of wonder and deep privilege.

A similar experience happened yesterday morning – seventy years hence. I was sitting at my kitchen table when a grey bird a bit larger than a robin flew onto the iron railing of my front porch. It remained there several moments and flew down onto the evergreen shrub to feed on the red berries. It kept looking nervously about because of my presence. I identified it as a mockingbird and watched it fly off, displaying its characteristic white wing patches. While most of the summer birds have left for warmer climes, with the warming of the northern winters, the mockingbird, robin, blue bird and other birds tend to remain. My feeling this morning seeing the mockingbird was virtually the same as that of the young lad in Scout camp – it was a "privileged moment."

BUTTERFLY WING AND A BLACK UMBRELLA

I found the wing of a Monarch butterfly. It was so exquisite, so delicate – orange with veins of black. I could only think, that encapsulated in the wing segment were tales of long flights to southern climes. But where to put it so as not to damage its gossamer delicateness? I was carrying a large, folded, black, men's umbrella. I gently inserted the half-wing between the folds of the umbrella. The delicate trophy made it home safely and undamaged.

WELCOME, FEATHERED FRIENDS, TO OUR BIRD HOUSE!

In the spring of 1992, at our Richmond Shores cottage, a curious drama took place at a bird-house we had attached to a tree. A Hairy Woodpecker had appeared and was hammering on the box. Believing it was trying to enlarge the entrance-hole, we took the house down and obligingly enlarged the hole to accommodate our guest. But, mysteriously, it kept up the pecking – and not even at the opening. The loud, staccato drumming echoed through the Shores. After consulting an ornithologist, we learned the drumming of the Hairy Woodpecker was a mating ritual. The bird had no intention of occupying the box. A few days passed and we observed a pair of birds hovering around the box. To our pleasant surprise, they were Crested Flycatchers. Would they choose our box? When they disappeared, we thought the site was not secluded enough for these deep-forest birds. Then, to our utter delight, they returned and began laying in the nesting material.

In the meantime, we learned the Crested Flycatcher has the curious and inexplicable habit of weaving a cast-off snake skin in its nest. We would bide our time until the fledglings were grown and the nest evacuated before checking the contents. In the meantime, we indulged ourselves, observing our feathered guests coming and going with beaks laden with insects for their hungry charges. At the end of the summer, we took down the box, emptied its contents and, wonder of wonders, found the snake-skin, woven in among the nesting material

One could say this drama fulfilled a life-long dream. When we were young, we used to laboriously construct crude bird houses out of orange crates dragged from the corner grocery store. Our tools were primitive but we labored with childlike hopefulness. Living in the inner city, all we could expect was the common English sparrow. Now, in our adulthood, we were privileged to have our bird house selected by the wonderful and elusive Crested Flycatchers.

BIRDERS SHOULD BECOME VEGETARIANS

I wrote the following letter in response to an article in *Birdscope* titled "Replaceable Wilderness":

In the forties, I would frequent Washington Park in Albany, when the spring, migratory warblers were abundant. In those days I would meet Dr. Dayton Stoner, New York State Zoologist, who was gathering notes for his book, *"The Birds of Washington Park."* Now, still birding, I am hard put to sight migratory warblers in my favorite haunt, The Five Rivers Environmental Center outside of Albany. I realize your focus is the North American boreal forest but I would make the following comment: The depletion of the Amazon rain forests to provide grazing land for cattle is also responsible for our declining migratory bird population. The very place that is a refuge for the birds we love is being destroyed to feed the American appetite for hamburgers whose principal providers are McDonalds and Burger King. Birders should be encouraged to become vegetarians.

"Thinginess"

Many long for a life of simplicity. "Thinginess" is a cloud that obscures spirituality. Pirke Avot teaches: "The more possessions the more worries" (2:8). I would add, 'The more possessions, the less spirituality."

"Of the Earth"

Walking recently on my favorite country road, I felt free, alive and protected. Free of technology and human artifice – except for my attire, an industrial product. Alive because I was moving on my own power and breathing the wonderfully healing country air. Protected because I was in my "true home" – under the luminous blue dome of the heavens. One of the deficits of modern civilization is our separation from our source, the earth. To be truly and fully human is to be connected to our origin. Much of our emotional discrepancy stems from this disconnect. "Man is of the earth, earthy." We are Adam – from the Hebrew *adamah* – earth.

Sounds

The voice is the fingerprint of the soul. Sounds are my life – nature's sounds, the sounds of the liturgy, and the sounds of children. Birding depends on sound-recognition.

One hears a bird's song and seeks it out. The birder's ear is keen. Sadly, most people walk through nature and miss nature's song.

"INTENTIONAL LIVING"

Most of us live our lives, following whatever the day brings. Others live *intentionally, initiating* meaningful activities and experiences. Our rabbis teach, "*Mitzvah goreret mitzvah*" – Freely rendered, 'One meaningful act often leads to another meaningful act.'

I was sitting at home one Shabbat afternoon when I began thinking, "Where is the meaning? I should betake myself to the synagogue for the minchah afternoon prayers." As I approached the synagogue, I caught a glimpse of familiar figures on an opposite corner. My friend Fran was accompanying her husband who was in a motorized wheel chair with their son Mitchell walking along side. Mitchell is the young man who had gone with me several weeks before to photograph birds at Five Rivers. Mitchell, whom I had taught for bar-mitzvah, was entering his junior year of college. Fran's faithful devotion to her husband, immobilized for many years with a spinal affliction, was deeply moving. I waited on the corner for the family to cross the busy New Scotland Avenue intersection, whereupon pleasant conversation ensued. I suggested Mitchell might like to accompany me again for another bird-photography opportunity at Five Rivers. He agreed. I arrived Sunday morning at Mitchell's house at 9 AM, expecting him to appear with all his photographic gear. When he approached with only a small pair of 7 x 20 pocket binoculars – a gift from his bar-mitzvah – I asked where his camera was. H replied he just wanted to enjoy bird-watching without the encumbrance of photographic paraphernalia. The photographer, we agreed, is so intent on technology he often is cheated out of the experience of the moment.

It was a languid, hazy morning but the birds were active. We sighted a wren that had occupied a hole in an old apple tree and another wren that had taken over a blue-bird house and was making sorties to feed its progeny. I explained wrens typically inhabit pre-made structures rather than fashion open nests in trees.

We enjoyed following a gaggle of Canada Geese that were waddling in front of us on the path and finally turned off into the pond. We were fascinated at how they stayed in line, even in the water – reminiscent of the V-formation-flight patterns in the high skies during migration. They have this unique trait of "following the leader."

Mitchell was particularly impressed with a Cedar Waxwing and remarked how silken its feathered pattern is. We observed Cardinals, Song-Sparrows, Red-Winged Blackbirds and finally were alerted by a loud, strident "skewk" from across the pond. Mitchell jokingly remarked, "It must be a Pterodactyl!" It was, in fact, a Green Heron which had flown across the pond, pursued by a smaller bird.

The one downside of the morning was the incessant, black flies swarming around our heads. I suggested to Mitchell it might be his hair shampoo. He vowed not to use shampoo before the next bird-walk. I cut a small pine branch for Mitchell to use as a switch to fend off the flies. It was good birding with this sensitive, appreciative young man who has now been "infected" for life.

All this was the outcome of picking my self up from a

"meaningless" afternoon and setting out for the synagogue. It is not enough to just "live." We need to *initiate* meaningful acts. Truly, 'one meaningful act brings another in its train.'

27

Illness Humanizes

Illness lays one low and the world is viewed differently. The difference is not only physical; it also is spiritual. Friends visit and, from a prone position, faces seem more compassionate, more beautiful. But the beauty and compassion were ever present; they simply were not sensed. Was it because the rush of life didn't permit it; the pressing (often imagined) duties of the hour did not let the heart focus; the mind's camera raced across jewels of human experience and wonder became elusive? But in the hospital bed there are no pressing duties. All things come into focus. The world is fashioned anew; the window of the soul is opened and light floods the heart.

Those who come to visit also are changed; through extending compassion are transformed. The giver and the recipient are linked by the act of compassion and an almost pure understanding flows between them. Some mystic equalizer erases status. This happens when the student comes to visit the teacher. In the classroom and school corridor, there is roll-playing. Deeper feelings are controlled and obscured; affections are held in check. But now emotions flow naturally and unaffectedly between them. Thereafter, it is never quite the same between them.

Suffering humanizes. One who has not suffered cannot fully share the sorrow of another sufferer. One may go through the ritual of sympathy but it may be only a token expression. But having suffered oneself, the pain of others is more tangibly felt. This is a blessing that flows from illness.

One lies for days in a hospital room, excluded and deprived. Birds flutter and soar freely outside; trees bend in the wind; children frolic and call joyously to each other; squirrels playfully chase each other up and down tree limbs. One beholds this and waits for someone to bring him a portion thereof. It is a great kindness and significant human act to do so.

28

Death's Poignant Lesson

"*It is better to go to the house of mourning than to go to the house of feasting . . . for the living shall lay it to heart*" (*Ecclesiastes 7:2*). *Death is the ultimate reminder of life's brevity and urgency. There is no urgency in eternity but only in our brief, mortal span.*

Eulogy for Martha Picker, May 5, 2003.

A time-honored Jewish tradition on Friday night at the *Kiddush* table is for the husband to recite the *Eshet chayil* to his wife: "A woman of valor, who can find? Her price is far above rubies" (Proverbs 31:10—31). Jewish husbands dutifully and lovingly sing this ode to their wives.

At this time, I ask forgiveness of my beloved wife for failing in this *mitzvah*. But, in my wife's absence, and in her memory, I shall do so. Husbands, I commend this worthy and loving practice to you. If not in Hebrew, recite the words in English. Do not wait until your *Eshet Chayil is* taken from you to tell her how precious she *was.*

The rabbis refer to the Jewish wife as the *bayit* – the home. It is the wife who sanctifies the home when she kindles the Sabbath lights, bringing light into the darkness of the work-a-day week. It is the wife who enables us to fulfill one of the great *mitzvot* of Judaism – *hachnasat orchim* – receiving guests at the Shabbat table. As the soul is to the body, so the wife is to the home. Without her, the house is but an empty shell — mere walls. How sad and regretful we do not know this until our precious jewel is removed from us! How sad! Blessed are they who know and blessed are their families.

You who loved Martha will best memorialize her by emulating her kindness, patience and forgiving spirit. Her life was a blessing and her memory shall be a blessing.

The sweet lips that sang are still. The heart that loved is quiet. The hands that made those magical meals no longer move. But the memories linger on. . . . . Sleep restfully, my sweet. . . .

29

Timeliness in the House of Mourning

The *mitzvah* of *nichum avelim* – 'comforting mourners' – is an important *gemilut chesed* – 'act of loving-kindness' – one that requires sensitivity and timing. The sage of Ecclesiastes taught, "To every thing there is a season and a time to every purpose under heaven – a time to weep and a time to laugh" (3:1-4). I question whether what often transpires in the house of mourning on the part of visitors is timely. We visit the house of mourning to comfort the mourners, not to regale ourselves. We overstay when mourners are heavy of heart and weary of body.

"It is better to go into the house of mourning than the house of feasting . . . for the living shall lay it to heart" (Ecclesiastes 7:2). Too often the house of mourning is transformed into a house of feasting and socializing. This is not timely.

When hearts are tender and open to be inspired, it is not a time to rush through the prayers but a time to impart Jewish values. We create a prayerful mood by chanting familiar prayers together.

Pirke Avot teaches, "Silence is a fence to wisdom . . . Say little and do much." When comforting mourners, say little and listen much. The sensitive ear, sympathetic heart and warm embrace are all that are needed.

"There is a time for everything under the sun" and the wise of heart understand timeliness.

30

Eulogy for Irving Yitzhak Vics
(June 25, 1978)

Irving Yitzhak Vics, O.D., was my friend. Ours was an "early-morning" friendship, as it were. We were fellow bird-watchers – "amateur ornithologists," as Irving liked to call us – two comrades who walked quietly, side by side, in rhythm with the pure, washed morning world.

We rose with the dawn, before the clang and clatter of the work-a-day. We learned to look up and away from material things. Our morning bird-walks were spiritual experiences which strengthened our friendship and renewed our kinship with nature.

Irving was an accomplished practitioner of his profession, highly respected among his colleagues. Yet he could betake himself to the park at 6:00 A.M., stand beneath a tree, binoculars poised and focused on a tiny bird, feeling for all the world like a child overcome with wonder. This ability to wonder child-like was one of his most precious qualities. The Creator Himself must surely have taken similar delight in His creative works. How odd, Irving and I often mused, that men stand in awe before museum masterpieces but do not see the living masterpieces of nature that daily surround us.

Below is a short literary piece created several years ago by Irving Vics:

THE BIRD KINGDOM

By I. Irving Vics, Amateur Observer

"As the first silvery glow of dawn ascends gently over the horizon, the High Priest of the bird kingdom heralds the birth of the new day, with a clear, melodious, musical trill. At first his song is genteel and sweet. It is a rhyme of reverence; it is a song of thanks; it is a melody of prayer. And then he waits for the congregation to arise and join him in the spiritual supplication service. But there is no response.

"As a *Kohen*, the Cardinal is short of temper, the historically known characteristic of *Kohanim*, and his song becomes louder, and quickened and more vibrant. He sings mightily. Finally there is an awakening among his congregants.

"A song is heard from the north, another from the south, and in a short time there are several voices. Soon there is a minyan, and then almost instantly the entire congregation is heard in full throated songs of prayer. The morning devotion of thanks to the Almighty is rousing and lusty and beautiful. This is not cacophony but a fully orchestrated symphony. This is the morning prayer, the *Shacharit*."

"The service is ended and each flies in search of his favorite break-fast. The remainder of the day is spent in the conglomerate of activities dear to the hearts of each individual species. And with the coming of dusk, when the sun has lowered its glowing beauty below the horizon, the *Kohanim* call to all to sing the songs of *Maariv*. Then all is quiet.

"As in all groups, whether human, bird or animal, there always is the exception to the rule. Mayhap this is good. In the bird kingdom the exception is the Mockingbird. Someone must have told him that he had been chosen as the official state bird of the great State of Florida. His enthusiasm for this honor knows no bounds, for he not only engages wholeheartedly in the *Shacharit* and *Maariv* prayers, but continues singing throughout the entire nighttime of darkness – every hour on the hour."

[I concluded my eulogy with the following:]

Irving, in July of 1975, you wrote me from Florida that you were trying to find someone who could accompany you on bird trips. You now have the best possible partner – your beloved Esther. Together you can observe all the glories of God's creation. Happy bird-watching, dear friend!

31

Bat Mitzvah Talk to Shoshanna Strumfeld
(May 3, 2003)

Several years ago, when your parents asked me to be your teacher, to prepare you for this special day, they gave me a gift. And what a precious gift you have been!

Shoshanna — your name means rose. When you first came to me, you were a tender rosebud. During the past two years, as you have grown, matured and prepared for this special day, the rosebud has blossomed into a lovely rose. I have been privileged to nurture this precious flower — but not I alone. The primary nurturers have been you wise and caring parents and your brother David.

As your teacher, my role has been a sacred one. According to our sages, "He who teaches Torah to the son or daughter of his fellow man is as though he had begotten that one." Indeed, if the Torah is a "Tree of Life," then imparting Torah is imparting the gift of life — life for the student and life for the people Israel. I thank God for the privilege of imparting to you the Torah of life, for its "ways are ways of pleasantness and all its paths are peace" (Proverbs 3:17).

The Torah is a tree of life for the Jewish People and you, as a woman, have a special role to play. In Judaism, a child's religion is determined by the mother. The mother's spiritual influence on the child is significant. The transmission of the Jewish heritage by the mother has been symbolized by the pitcher of water carried by our mother Rivkah at the well.

The Jewish mother bears the life-giving waters of Torah. You, my dear Shoshanna, are a link in the chain of Jewish tradition.

You are now a *bat-mitzvah* – daughter of commandment.' Last night, at Kabbalat-Shabbat, you fulfilled the mitzvah of kindling the Shabbat lights. Until you lit those candles, they were lifeless. When you added flame to the candles, you brought them to life. Your flame was your love. As you gathered their light toward you, lovingly encircling them with your hands, you were embracing the Torah and the people of Israel.

My dear Shoshanna, the preservation of the Torah and the people of Israel are in your hands. May the Sabbath lights ever illumine your Sabbath table and may your life shine with the love of Torah and deeds of loving kindness.

32

Wedding Talk to Phil and Anna
(May 29, 2006)

The Friday before last, as I lit the Shabbat candles and sang *eshet chayil*, 'woman of valor,' to my departed wife and angel Martha, *aleha hashalom*, I thought the *eshet chayil* embodies the best teachings I could impart to you today at this *chuppa kedushin*.

The sage of Proverbs wrote *eshet chayil* over 2500 years ago. How wise of the rabbis to have the husband recite it every Friday night to his wife.

"A woman of valor, who can find? Her price is far above rubies. The heart of her husband trusts in her." Pinchas, you have found the priceless woman of valor and Channa, you have found the priceless man of valor. You are beginning your lives together with mutual trust – the key to marital love and harmony.

"She renders him good and not evil all the days of her life." – She never speaks ill of him and supports all his endeavors.

"All the days of her life . . . ." – She is a constant source of strength and character.

"She seeks wool and flax and works willingly with her hands. She rises while it is yet night and provides sustenance for her household." – She is a *true baalat habayit* – "mistress of her house," who looks well to the material and spiritual needs of her household.

"Her lamp goes not out at night." – Spiritual meaning: Her faith, hope and love are constant and burn brightly, even during the darkness of illness, tragedy and misfortune.

"She extends her hand to the poor and needy." – Friends and strangers will always be found at her table.

"Her husband is known in the gates when he sits among the elders of the land." – Her husband's good name is enhanced by her character and good deeds.

"Strength and dignity are her clothing." – Virtue and goodness, not outward appearance, define her character.

"She opens her mouth with wisdom and the Torah of loving kindness is on her tongue." – She is gentle of heart and imparts the wisdom of Torah by word and deed.

"Her children rise up and call her blessed, her husband also and he praises her." – Her family blesses her because she has blessed them. She is strengthened and comforted by her husband's praise.

"Charm is deceitful and beauty is vain; but a woman that fears the Lord – she shall be praised." – When, in the waning years of life, physical beauty shall fade, her inner beauty will still remain.

Whereas *eshet chayil* would appear to focus on the virtuous woman, by implication it must include the virtuous man – for only a man of virtue would choose a woman of virtue.

My dear Pinchas – recite the eshet chayil to your wife every Shabbat, after she has kindled the Shabbat lights. It will bring joy to her, provide an example to your children and be an ever-present reminder of your treasured *eshet chayil,* Channa.

I commend to you both the Friday night Shabbat ritual, as a formula for a loving Jewish home:

We light the Shabbat candles.

We bless the children.

We greet the Shabbat angels.

We bless the wife.

We sanctify the Shabbat over wine.

We bless the Shabbat loaves.

In fulfilling the above, your home will be a *Gan Eden* – a garden of delight. This is my prayer and blessing for you on this joyful day of your *Chuppa Kedushin*.

33

Searching for our Ancestors

"Children's children are the crown of old men;
and the glory of children are their fathers" (Proverbs 17:6)

*[A talk at Temple Israel, April 28, 1970, introducing
The Family Tree: The Descendants of Velvel Pochapovsky,
Horodyszcze, White Russia. He was my paternal great-great
grandfather.]*

As a young man, family was not too important to me.
When my uncle would tell me, "Blood is thicker than
water," I had no notion of what he meant. Now family is
precious to me. A year ago I attended the funeral of this
uncle and spoke with his brother, a convert to Christianity. I
later wrote the following to my uncle:

"*Zecher tsadik livracha*" – The memory of the righteous
is for a blessing" (Proverbs 10:7). Human beings are less
affected by people who moralize than by moral people. The
remembrance of my dear grandparents and their gentleness,
modesty, piety and love has taught me more than books or
sermons. I still remember the small purse grandmother kept
in her kitchen, into which she would deposit coins for some
itinerant, needy soul. I remember, as a young boy, when
she had me take a few pennies down to an old man. Her
concern for those less fortunate than she – and she herself
was not too well off – was little understood by me then. But

how I love this virtuous soul now when I recall her deeds of loving-kindness! Truly, her memory is a blessing.

Does love stop at the grave? Our rabbis ask: Which is greater: *tsedakah* (charity), or *gemilut chasadim* (deeds of loving-kindness)? Their answer – *gemilut chasadim*. Charity is for the living whereas deeds of loving-kindness may be performed for the living or the dead. Faithfulness to the dead is completely gratuitous – they cannot thank us. In Judaism, honoring the dead is among the most altruistic of human expressions.

In my search for information about my family, I visited a nearby cemetery. To my sadness, I found gravestones toppled and graves overgrown. This was not necessarily from vandalism. They were old and time had taken its toll. I could only think they were the memorials of someone's grandparents or great-grandparents. They were uncared for and forgotten.

Earlier this year my cousin, her husband and their two daughters visited us. After taking them on a tour of the city, I took them to visit the grave of our grandfather. My cousin had never seen it. She later wrote me her children were full of questions about their family and she was grateful for the experience.

When a kindness has been done to us, is it not ingratitude to forget? I have inquired after my ancestors and relatives so they shall not be forgotten. My search originally was spurred by curiosity – I wanted to know who I was. Can one truly know oneself without knowing one's flesh-and-blood antecedents? Are we not all part of those who preceded us? Is there not in each of us a bit of a father, mother, grandparent or great-grandparent? I often thought longingly of the beautiful souls who had died, taking their precious knowledge of family to the grave – an irreclaimable and lamentable loss! The family book will insure the perpetuation of some of this precious knowledge.

My search began here in Albany, where we are privileged to have elderly cousins who are links with the past. With insatiable curiosity, as I sat and talked with these dear, venerable souls, it was like unearthing hidden treasures. Each name I discovered was like a precious jewel and I hoarded these jewels until I had amassed a veritable treasure.

Ours is a big and impersonal world, teeming with people – often lonely people. In our mobile society, families are separated and lose touch with one another. What a great loss! I had been told of a cousin in Texas, a Psychiatrist. The last communication with him had been in 1930. I tracked this elusive cousin through many states – from his internship, to his residency and, finally, to his appointment as chief of Mental Hygiene at the V. A. Hospital in Waco, Texas. He wrote that since his father had died when he was only eight months old, he knew very little about his family. How great was his joy at receiving knowledge of his father's family!

The knowledge of our ancestors and relatives is a source of inspiration. To know them is to want to continue their noble lives and dreams. Our Jewish heritage takes on added preciousness when we behold the many before us of our own flesh and blood who held it precious. To be ignorant of family is to be cheated out of one of life's greatest rewards. Let not your children be so cheated. Tell them about their family. Take them to the burial places of their beloved relatives and read to them the inscriptions on those memorials.

The Talmud relates the following tale: Honi Ha-m'agel was walking along the way when he beheld a man planting a Carob. Inquired Honi: "How many years will it take for this tree to bear fruit?" "Seventy years," replied the man. "And are you certain you will be alive in seventy years to eat its fruit?" asked Honi. Answered the man: "I found the world with Carobs. As my fathers planted for me, so I plant for my children" (Taanit, 23).

[*Postscript: My fathers and mothers planted for me by keeping Torah alive and bequeathing it to me. Now it is my obligation and privilege to keep their memories and their righteous deeds alive for the blessing of future generations. The Mishneh teaches, "It is not incumbent upon you to complete the work; neither are you free to desist from it" (Pirke Avot 2:21). Though I started the work of the family tree, I surely could not finish it; it is a never-ending story. But I am privileged that others in the family are inspired to carry it on. This is all I could have hoped for.*]

34

"Raise up Many Students"
(Pirke Avot 1:1)

[*From the author's book,* Students Discover Genesis, *1975*]

A notorious shortcoming of teachers, often because of preoccupation with lesson plans, is the failure to listen to what their students are saying. Even more problematical is getting students to speak up at all. Teachers naturally are proficient in their subject and in their eagerness to present it, dominate the classroom. The result is students either do not have the opportunity to speak or are too timid to match wits with the austere figure before them. To get students to "open up" requires a measure of humility on the part of the teacher. One must sincerely believe that 'he who is wise learns from everyone' (Pirke Avot 4:1) – and this includes the young! Student spontaneity and candor are discouraged when the impression is conveyed that we are "fishing" for specific answers. We do this by politely setting aside comments that do not fit our preconceptions. A hard lesson for a teacher to learn is that the *student is more important than the subject;* that the learning-*process* pre-empts the material. As the student makes discoveries in the text, he simultaneously makes discoveries about *himself.* He tastes the sweetness of literary analysis, and learning is no longer drudgery but is exciting and fulfilling. The student's self-image improves. He senses that he – a young person – is also capable of significant thinking. The climate for discovery is created when teacher and student search for meaning *together,* with all the answers not there from the beginning. Teachers do not have all the answers anyway but, unfortunately, they are reluctant to confess this and so practice the art of dissimulation. Seeking to protect their image, teachers believe it would be calamitous if they were found not to be *infallible!* After all, would this not shatter the students' confidence in the teacher as an authority-figure! Should a student produce an answer the teacher did not have and which might actually change the teacher's opinion, the wise and sensitive teacher will honestly acknowledge it and stand corrected. In this kind of candid atmosphere, a student will feel that he is not merely a recipient of someone else's ideas but he too can make a valid contribution. He too is a person! [Rashi, the greatest Jewish biblical commentator, when confronted with a question he could not answer, candidly admitted, "I do not know."]

A key to learning is the *right question,* not the *right answer,* as many think. A climate must be created in the classroom that encourages students to ask hard questions. It is a grave error to attempt to ask questions that have not yet been asked. There is nothing so irrelevant for a young student as an answer without a question.

[Note: *The author's book, published in 1975, is a compilation of over two-thousand questions and comments of his students, solicited by the following method: A chapter of Genesis was read to the class in contemporary English, after which the students would re-read the chapter, recording any questions they might have. They were encouraged to write freely and candidly -- which often consumed most of the class-period. Their questions and comments were collated and typed out by verse, with the student's names. At the next session, each student received a copy of the cumulative comments of the class, followed by a period of excitement as the students eagerly scanned their papers for their comments in print. The day's lesson revolved around their questions, with maximum participation. Their questions and comments were saved and printed in a book.*]

35
Jewish Day School—
Counter Culture Institution

Address, Bet Shraga Hebrew Academy
September 23, 1999]

The Jewish Day School is a citadel in a world embattled. Goodness, kindness, fairness and truth are under siege. The most powerful educational tools every devised by man – television and the computer – are more often motivated by material gain than justice, truth and morality. Standing astride the breach is the Jewish Day School, guided by the principle enunciated by the prophet Micah: "Do justly, love kindness" (Micah 6:8).

The Jewish Day School is "counter-culture," that is, counter pop-culture – the prevailing culture which appeals mostly to the "yetzer hara," the baser human instincts. The Jewish Day School seeks to counteract the "yetzer hara" with a most potent antidote – Torah. In the broader sense, Torah encompasses the entire corpus of Jewish wisdom, created over millennia by wise teachers possessed of keen insight into the human situation. Torah is one of the most humane value-systems devised by man.

Albany's Bet Shraga Hebrew Academy has an enclave called the "Shomre-Torah Society," comprised of large-hearted women and men of vision – the "Guardians of Torah." The Torah is not an inanimate object to be guarded electronically, but a living, dynamic entity. It is well characterized by the symbolism "Etz Chaim," 'Tree of Life.' Like a tree, the Torah grows, has roots, bears fruit and provides benefits. We guard the Torah by ensuring the perpetuation of its value-system and establishing institutions that teach its values. When Torah is taught in an environment of love, it results in the propagation of more living "trees of life" – Jewish students who love and live Torah.

When I recently had occasion to discuss tonight's meeting with Fran Waldman, a Bet Shraga parent, her insightful responses so moved me that I asked her to record them:

"We send our children to Bet Shraga because we see it as a partner in building the foundation that will help them grow into moral and compassionate human beings. Bet Shraga reinforces the morals and values we try to instill in our children, giving them the sense of pride and identify so important in developing their self-confidence. It shows them the beauty of their history, the sacrifices of their ancestors and the blessings, joys and occasional sorrows that come with living a Jewish life. Finally, we are giving our children the Jewish education we never had – the fulfillment of our personal dreams. There is no guarantee our children will lead Jewish lives or marry Jewish mates, but some day they may be able to make an educated choice. If they choose to move away from Judaism, they will have the foundation of knowledge to enable them to return."

36

Philip Shraga Arian (1929–1972)

Philip Shraga Arian was principal of the Hebrew school of Temple Israel, Albany, New York, from 1957 to 1971 and founding director of the Bet Shraga Hebrew Academy. Following his untimely death in 1972, I was privileged to compile a memorial volume of his speeches and writings entitled, *He Kindled a Light*.

Philip Shraga Arian was a nationally renowned educator par excellence. It was he who inspired me to enter Jewish education and was my teacher, role model and principal. My educational philosophy largely coincides with and was greatly influenced by him. Above I cited the mishnaic passage, "Raise up many students." Philip Shraga Arian fulfilled this wonderfully. He not only "raised up," that is, taught many students, he literally *raised* them up, inspiring and motivating many of them to become educators themselves.

In the closing chapter of the book, *He Kindled a Light,* I wrote the following in the form of a letter to my late friend, colleague and teacher: [I have slightly altered the original wording.]

"The Other morning, when our children were praying in the *Bet Midrash* [small synagogue], we looked out across the spacious field in back of the Academy and saw the trees swaying in the wind. They seemed to be dancing and we were caught up with joy as we felt their joy – and then we remembered how you used to dance during *tefillah* [prayer-service.] How you would have loved sharing that experience with us! And that great, majestic white pine that stands alone in the field like a silent watchman – how you would have loved that tree! Is there the slightest doubt you would have had us praying under its fragrant boughs when the weather turned warm!

"We took the children into the woods the other day and came across an injured tree. We scraped off the loose bark and daubed the wound with pitch so the tree could heal itself. You would have immediately caught the relevance of what we were doing.

"Several weeks before the festival of Chanukah, we found a fallen birch in the woods and mused, 'What a pity such a thing of beauty should just rot away!' We wondered what to do with it and then an idea flashed into our minds: Make it into a Chanukah menorah! Every time we look at the menorah, with its white and blue candles casting their warm glow in the wondering eyes of children and the wax mingling as it drips down on the white birch-bark, we can only picture how ecstatic you would have been over this piece of fantasy which ignited the hearts of children.

"You left us too soon. We miss your inspiring counsel but we remember what Pirke Avot teaches us: 'In the place where there are no men, endeavor to be a man' (2:6). When you were here, you were the man. Now that you are gone, we must be the man. Not an easy task. But lest our love for you become mere sentiment, we must carry on the work you started. As long as there is power within us, we shall always guard your final admonition: 'Take care of things while I am gone.'"

37

Address at Educators Assembly

Presenting the book, *He Kindled a Light*
Concord Hotel, March 21, 1976

What was the greatness of the man call Shraga Arian? Why have we troubled to come here? Is it a mere exercise in nostalgia? Who are the people who came to honor the memory of Shraga Arian? Who are Sanford Sheber, Devorah Heckelman, Gina Pearl and Chaim Picker? People whose lives were profoundly touched by Shraga Arian; who share his passion for Jewish survival. We came to tell of a man whose philosophy was right for Jewish survival. We came because we believe his philosophy is desperately needed by Jews today. We came because our hearts ache for the hundreds of thousands of Jewish children who have been lost to Judaism.

What was the greatness of this man? I shall not dare to try to capture it in a few minutes. But I will attempt to give you a glimpse; then urge you to study his life. Listen to his spontaneous comments at a meeting of Camp Givah parents:

"Most people still think of Judaism as something narrow, something you do in shul, or at home, with kosher dishes. They don't see that Judaism involves a whole approach to life. Camp Givah is much more than a Jewish camp. Or, it is a Jewish camp – if you understand what Judaism is. One of the main things we are trying to do with these children is give them a sense of awareness – awareness about the things around them. We feel a Jew is a human being who does not take life for granted. And I am not referring to physical things. I am talking about the song, 'The Best Things in Life Are Free.' It's trite but it happens to be true. Our aim is to try to make these children aware of the glorious things around them – nature, God, personal relationships, pain, humor, laughter. You know, when you get right down to it, what is a human being left with after all the things he has amassed; after all the success? He is left with himself. If we can teach these children to be secure alone, to know this world was made for them, then we shall feel we have given them something."

In an orientation talk to Camp Givah counselors, Shraga Arian said: "The first day of camp is important. You're scared. All of us are. It's stage fright. If *we* have stage fright, imagine what the kid who has to wait for that bus must be feeling. The bus is late. He finally gets on, sits in a seat, sees strange people. It's a horrible feeling. Make him feel at home. A smile, a touch on the hair – whatever you can do. First impressions are very important. There is nothing worse than getting on a bus and seeing cold, hard faces."

Shraga Arian spoke of creativity in human relationships: "Creativity is not only in traditional, artistic forms. I've learned that the group can be a creative form; that there is a certain beautiful creativity in groups of people coming together and doing something no one else can do as well; that a group which is artistically orchestrated can be such a creative force. I found that in a family called Camp Givah.

"People are hungry to get caught up in the uniqueness of being human. They want to sing, to dance, to relate. They want to believe, to count. You bless someone when you give them this gift.

"I've learned that when all the assemblies and all the camps and all the schools and all the mass meetings are over, the most important thing left is the one-to-one relationship. All these structures exist so we can focus on the one-to-one relationship. There is a song that will forever haunt me: 'The days turn, the year passes, but what remains for ever is the melody, the music, the havershaft—that special something between precious friends."

And what was that precious something with which Shraga Arian blessed us? He enabled us to express our humanity in a unique, Jewish way. The people here know what I mean. They will tell you. I was one of those who Shraga Arian affected in a creative Jewish way, for a higher purpose. Eighteen years ago, he lured me from behind a merchandise counter, introducing me to a world in which my stock in trade was Torah and my patrons were children. The Arian memorial volume is our way of saying thank you.

The title of the book, *He Kindled a light*, was thoughtfully chosen. It alludes to Shraga's name which means "light." His life was luminous, kindling the fire of Judaism in countless hearts – fires which still burn brightly. It is no coincidence Shraga loved candles. He knew the mystic power of a flickering candle to arouse wonder and awe in children and adults. What is there about a flame that reminds us of Shraga? A flame sheds light and warmth. This was Shraga. Some who did not fully understand him, or rather, did not know him intimately, remember him only for his wild antics – his "Africa," his masquerading, his lusty singing. What a pity! These were but a means to an end. Through these devices, he enthralled his students – and having done so, led them to the fountain to drink; to drink Torah, the Jewish classics and the mitzvot.

It is related in Tractate Taanit that the sage Rav had a fish pond. When a student balked at coming to learn, he "bribed" him by promising to let him fish in his pond—until finally he got the student to study. Shraga lured his students to Torah with Shabbat stories, Melavei Malka, Jewish salami, Camp Givah and bear-hugs.

Shraga Arian knew how vital it is to feed the emotions and the senses. But above all, he fed the mind. His probing honesty and insatiable curiosity were contagious and his students caught his passion and were turned on to the Jewish classics.

Shraga Arian was a dreamer. The prophets were dreamers. God does not make many dreamers. To dream is Jewish – to dream of a better world and a greater potential for man and society. The prophet is the eyes of the people. Shraga Arian showed us dreams. Through his eyes we beheld visions.

"The path of the righteous is as a shining light that shines ever more brightly until the perfect day" (Proverbs 4:18). Shraga Arian was a shining light in our lives; a light that still burns brightly. May the light he kindled go on shedding warmth and understanding in the minds and hearts of Jews, both old and young, and may the light of Judaism never be extinguished.

38

Address, Tribute Dinner, Temple Israel
(June 10, 1990)

Tonight's event is referred to as a "Tribute" or "Testimonial" dinner. I am aware of the usual understanding of these terms; but permit me to suggest an additional meaning.

When first approached about a possible dinner, I felt uncomfortable. After some gentle persuasion by my adorable cousin Barbara, however, I acquiesced. I think now I know why: Martha and I love our congregational family and this is our chance to tell you. Being very human and sentimental, we wanted to receive your massive, loving embrace. After all, who doesn't enjoy a huge hug!

So ... what is *my* meaning for "tribute" and "testimonial"? Simple! This is *our* tribute to *you* – *our* testimonial that *you* are the greatest! How impoverished our lives would have been without you! You have been our extended family, our support group, with whom we have shared joys and sorrows for 35 years.

I am reminded of the Talmudic tale of Honi the Circle-Maker, a saintly teacher of the first century, famed for his lucid replies to his students' questions . . . .

Once, while walking by the way, Honi happened upon a man planting a Carob tree. Asked Honi, "How many years will it take for this tree to bear fruit?" The man replied, "Seventy years." Honi continued, "And do you expect to be alive in seventy years to enjoy its fruit?" Replied the man,

"When I came into the world I found Carob trees . . . . As my fathers planted for me, so I plant for my children." Thereupon Honi sat down to eat and fell asleep. A huge boulder appeared, concealing him, and he slept for seventy years. Upon awakening, he saw someone eating the fruit of that very Carob tree. Asked Honi, "Are you the one who planted the tree?" "No," replied the man. "It was my grandfather!" Thought Honi, "I must have been asleep for seventy years!" Honi went to his house and asked the people," The son of Honi the Circle-Maker – where is he?" They replied, "He is dead; but there is a grandson!" Said Honi, "I am Honi the Circle-Maker!" But they disbelieved him. Thereupon Honi went to the House of Study and listened in on the sages who said, "This legal explanation is a clear as when Honi used to explain it! For when Honi used to enter the House of Study, he would elucidate the most difficult legal questions." Honi exclaimed, "I am Honi!" But they disbelieved him and did not accord him the honor he used to receive. Overcome with sadness, Honi besought mercy and expired. Rabba taught, this illustrates the saying: "Either friendship or death."

I cherish this story for two reasons: I love trees and I value friendship. Yes, dear friends, you are as important to us as life itself. What would our life be without you!

A little personal history: I was born in Albany, attended the Ferry Street Talmud Torah and the Heder of Mr. Isidore Aurbach. I was Bar Mitzvah in Beth-El Jacob synagogue on Herkimer Street. Three of my classmates in Mr. Aurbach's heder were our own Ida Zatz Leberman, her sister Tillie Zatz Grant and Evelyn Kahn Segel. I have a vivid recollection of them sitting in the row next to the window. Can you imagine what a privilege it was for me later to teach their children! Yes, and their grandchildren! Can you possibly imagine the pride I feel to be Hazzan in the shul of my childhood friends! It is a very special feeling.

A few more personal historical notes . . . . As a young

teenager I strayed from the faith of our fathers, only to rediscover my ancestral faith in the mid 1950's. It was a dear cousin who, in the fall of 1955, first encouraged me to come to a late-Friday night service in the newly built Temple Israel. I was timid and nervous and in need of moral support. She met me at the entrance and accompanied me into the service. That cousin was none other than the sweet mother of the gracious chairperson of this event – Sylvia Olshein.

This is how I once described my feelings upon attending my first service at Temple Israel: "The synagogue was unfamiliar and grandiose, so different from the modest down-town synagogue I had known in my youth. Although I was surrounded by people, I felt strange and alone. I had been away from the Jewish People too long . . . . The evening service began and the ark was opened, revealing the Torah scrolls, resplendent in their velvet mantles and silver crowns. As the Cantor intoned *Mah Tovu*, "How goodly are thy tents, O Jacob, thy tabernacles, O Israel," the estrangement left me and was replaced by a warm feeling of joy – a rapturous indescribable joy. After a fifteen-year sojourn in a strange land, I had returned home!"

During the growth-years of our family, it was our special privilege to be exposed in Temple Israel to exemplary human beings, whose virtues were an important influence in our lives. Rabbi Kieval warmly welcomed us into the Temple family. His late Friday night sermons were an inspiration and through his erudition and scholarship we were introduced to the literary treasures of our people. His love and respect for books were especially meaningful to me. Cantor Herbert Feder's deeply spiritual and melodious renditions of the prayers were a source of spiritual strength. I clearly remember how my heart was united with his heart as he chanted the prayers and I was transported to another realm, quite oblivious to my physical surroundings. Rabbi Leo and Shene Mordkoff were important role-models. Rabbi Mordkoff was the epitome of what a Jew ought to be -- pious yet tolerant; learned but not dogmatic, patiently encouraging those who attended the *minyan to* increase their knowledge and skills. It was under his concerned and watchful supervision I first led the prayers as a *baal tefillah*. I remember his patience with my halting and inexperienced manner. A Shabbat visit to the home of Shene and Leo Mordkoff was an inspirational experience. Its Jewish character was unmistakable – "Have a piece of cake or some fruit and make a *beracha*," they would say. Their Judaism was natural, not forced. Their loving devotion and piety were contagious.   Shraga Arian, a brilliant and gifted educator, was a friend, colleague and teacher, who gave me my first opportunity to teach in Temple Israel. His confidence inspired me to continually accept new challenges. One did not work *for* Shraga Arian but *with* him. I was privileged to be with him at the start of Camp Givah and the Hebrew Academy. Those were historic days, filled with excitement and challenge!

In November of 1962, at a home meeting for parents of the Temple's Gimel class (11-year olds), I discussed my philosophy of Jewish education: "A teacher must never lose sight of the grandeur and profound significance of the classroom experience. He must never let the mastery of skills and routine classroom management obscure the greater mission.   Each child is a future world citizen who has the potential to make a positive contribution – a big task in a little setting! A teacher prepares a child for life's problems and challenges – even tragedies. His students are young and impressionable. The teacher's role is consequential. The students are ever watching him for cues. The teacher must never ride roughshod over his pupil's feelings; never shame or embarrass them."

When, on another occasion, I was asked to explain the relevance of bird-watching to Hebrew education, I replied: "What business does a Hebrew teacher have in taking his class bird-watching at 6:00 A.M. in the morning? What does this have to do with Judaism? Those familiar with the rabbinical literature know that the rabbis were sensitive to nature. An appreciation for what God has created is intimately tied to Judaism. Consider the *berachot* one recites upon experiencing nature's wonders: Upon witnessing thunder or lightning, a great body of water, upon smelling a fragrant odor . . . ."

At a parents' night at Givah, I said: "America is the land of abundance. Advertising media bombard us with tempting things to buy. There is a tendency to seek pleasure in gadgets, in things. We must try to discover the simple, beautiful things of life – a tree, a flower, a bird – things money cannot buy. We need to develop a sense of wonder . . . . The world is so rich, so beautiful, by comparison with the glitter of the gadget-counters in the stores. There is good comradeship, hearty song. Choose a canoe over a speed boat. You glide along with hardly a whisper of noise as the paddle dips quietly in the water and you hear birds calling in the distance and you have time to notice the clouds wafting lazily overhead. This sensitivity, wonder, awe and independence from gadgets – this is what we are trying to instill in our Givah campers." This philosophy I shared in common with my dear friend, teacher and colleague Shraga Arian.

Rabbi Elimelech Paltiel Binyamin: A man of zeal passionately devoted to an authentic expression of Judaism. Without his tireless devotion, many wonderful aspects of Temple Israel might have fallen by the wayside – Camp Givah, Camp Horef, the Daily Minyan, Israeli Dance. Palti's greatest virtue is his sincere concern for people and their needs – both spiritual and physical. I have observed his tenderness with hospital patients, his comforting manner with mourners and his generosity to those with material needs. He is not one given to mere pious pronouncements from the pulpit but is a man of action, fulfilling the rabbinic virtue, *Emor m'at va-aseh harbeh*, "Say little and do much." Rabbi Silton's deep passion for justice involved him early on in the pursuit of Nazi war criminals. His love and devotion for the Jewish People is monumental, expressing itself most recently in his activism on behalf of Soviet Jews. Palti, without your encouragement I could not have achieved what I did as Hazzan. You suffered with my "growing pains," prodding me gently (sometimes not so gently) to do more. I owe you much for the wonderful experience of being Hazzan. Incidentally, I have not forgotten how you, Norm Rosenthal and Bill Rockwood kept urging me to accept the position of Hazzan. Your persuasive powers were irresistible.

There is another person – an unsung hero (no pun intended) – who was indispensable in my role as Hazzan. He is my dear and longtime friend, Cantor Dan Chick. Dan was my connecting link with the great Hazzanim. Before I had any thought of becoming a Hazzan, Dan would visit my home and sing famous cantorial pieces for me, accompanied by vignettes from the lives of the great cantors. When Dan was a boy he would visit shuls in New York where the great Cantors held forth and would sit enthralled, absorbing what he heard. His phenomenal musical memory served him well when he became a Cantor. Dan and Barbara, you have been precious friends, without whose encouragement I could not have accomplished my task.

Aharon aharon haviv – "*The* last is most beloved." Martha, you are my *eshet chayil,* my "woman of valor." Indeed, you have needed valor to endure me all these years. Concerning the woman of valor, Proverbs says, "The heart of her husband trusts in her. She renders him good and not evil all the days of his life. Her husband is known in the gates." Martha, all of this has been true of you. Our sages teach that a good name is much to be desired. I would add, a wife of good reputation is also greatly to be desired, for she brings honor and merit to her family. Martha, your good name and good works have brought honor to our family. The love and respect the community holds for you are known to all of us. You have been a good wife, caring mother and grandmother and a worthy Jew.

Dear friends, if I have achieved anything on the bimah of Temple Israel, it was not by my merit alone. You nurtured me with your warm friendship, encouragement and patience, as I learned my role. We grew together. When I became Hazzan, I was not yet sure of my role – overwhelmed as I was with the musical challenge. I gradually came to understand, however, that the Hazzan, true to the meaning of the Hebrew word, is primarily an "overseer" whose concern first and foremost should be the spiritual welfare of the congregation. I came to realize that my most important function would be as teacher, imparting synagogue skills, instilling Jewish pride, understanding and devotion. I came to understand that comforting the sick and bereaved and assisting those who attend the minyan were the areas of greatest significance. In a word, a Hazzan should be an enabler; for this is the role of an authentic teacher.

Dear friends, you have grown accustomed to my melodies and manner. Now there needs to be a period of transition. Just as you had to adjust to me, so will you adjust to my successor. "All beginnings are difficult." But there is great spirituality in this congregation and all will be well. Temple Israel will go from strength to strength.

A great labor of love has made this evening possible. Martha and I feel a deep sense of gratitude to our beautiful and selfless cousins Barbara and Elliot Wachs and the committee that assisted them. Finally, dear friends, thank you for all your loving messages which we shall cherish and for the gift of your presence tonight – a gift more precious than anything tangible you could have given us.

Permit me to close with *Yekum purkan* from the Shabbat morning service:

"May the blessings of Heaven – kindness and compassion, long life, ample sustenance, health, and healthy children who do not neglect the Torah – be granted to you. May the King of the universe bless you, adding to your days and your years. May you be spared all distress and disease. May our Father in Heaven be your help at all times. Amen"

39

Parting Remarks, Temple Israel
(June 23, 1990)

I wanted to take a few minutes to say – not farewell – but *l'hitraot* – 'until we meet again.' For you see, Martha and I feel an inseparable link to this congregation – our spiritual home for 35 years. We could never sever this bond.

Speaking, now, as a teacher . . . You entrusted your jewels – your children – to me and I received more than I gave. Mine was the sacred task of imparting to your children the heritage of Sinai – the knowledge of God and the love of Torah. I was constantly aware of the urgency of this assignment, for Judaism, you see, is a fragile plant, ever struggling for survival in a hostile and challenging environment. We the teachers of Judaism wage an unceasing battle to keep this fragile plant alive in the minds and hearts of our children. Only now, after years of effort, am I beginning to reap the harvest of my labors. Of late I have received numerous messages from former students, telling of the impact in their lives of our teaching.

What has this taught me? That there is an ingredient a teacher must have which supersedes all others: FAITH! – Faith that what we say and do vis-à-vis a student is never lost. We may encounter impassive faces, stubbornness and rebelliousness; but these must never dismay us and make us cynical. The seeds we sow in our children's hearts may lie dormant for years, only to germinate later. Our reward comes when we hear years later that we have changed a life.

I have spoken as a teacher of children. Now let me speak as Hazzan. Just as you have entrusted me with your children, so have you entrusted me with your hearts. As your *sheliach tsibur*, I have been your delegate in prayer before God. What a sacred trust and privilege you have granted me! When I have stood here on this bimah, between you and the *Shechinah* – the Divine Presence – I have not felt that mine was the only voice. My voice and heart were united with your voices and hearts in chorus and petition. This has been an indescribable privilege!

I have sometimes heard that the synagogue is devoid of spirituality. Those who charge this seek to justify their leaving us for another place. To the contrary, I have found spirituality, love and hope. I have found priceless souls and loving friends. I will conclude with a poem I wrote some twenty-five years ago, which was inspired by an experience at Camp Givah. I dedicate this poem to all the beautiful souls Martha and I have found in this congregation:

Meaning in a Heap of Stones -- Camp Givah, 1965

Seeking respite from the din -- and moments of mediation -- I followed the path back of the barn and up the hill. My teacher this day was to be a heap of stones . . . .

To this land that had never tasted the plowshare's blade, a hardy pioneer came, a hundred years ago or more, possessed of a dream . . . .

From early morn 'til twilight he toiled, to clear these acres of their rocky burden, wantonly strewn by the mountain of ice that eons ago had inexorably advanced here. Tediously, backbreakingly, he loaded rocks small and great on his stone sled and hauled them to a pre-chosen spot. His task completed, his plow would churn up the rich, black soil unchallenged.

The rock-heap remains, witness to a man's dauntless spirit,

fraught with history, telling a story of nature's reckless game and man's struggle to subdue earth and make it fruitful – waiting to teach a ready listener . . . .

When I came upon this rock-pile, I mused, "Mere rocks -- what unique thing can one discover in rocks?" Then I began to learn . . . .

People – how like a pile of rocks! The random look at the crowd reveals scant interest. At first undiscerning glance, people differ little nor hold much fascination . . . .

As I stood, staring at the heap of stones, I began to see more than at first, began to see *each* stone, each with its own character, its own colors; each with an interest exclusively its own. I examined one, then another, growing more wonder-filled at their variety and beauty . . . .

People – non-descript, perhaps, at first unthinking glance . . . .But look more closely and you will discover virtue and goodness undreamed of. Your search continued, you will turn up treasures untold . . . .

I searched among the rocks and came to one that excelled them all. Its virtue was inconspicuous, its beauty modestly hidden. I turned it over and over and found, in a remote corner, a minute impression, tiny as your fingernail, beautiful in its perfection, imprinted in its granite-like surface millennia ago. It was a fossil-imprint resembling a miniature sunburst . . .

And so are people – search among them and treasures will you unearth – as I did this day in a heap of stones, on the other side of the slope . . . .

40

Vignettes of Nature and other Musings

The Trail

(1965)

A walk through the forest among the tall sugar maples . . .

From the tops of the trees, the plaintive whistle of the Wood Pewee . . .

You pause, quietly waiting for him to whistle again . . .

It is still, except for the barely audible hum of tiny winged insects . . .

He whistles again and you continue on . . .

A fragile toadstool pokes up through the wet, decaying leaves . . .

You bend down to observe it more closely . . .

This modest plant of the forest floor . . .

You walk on, feeling exhilaration . . .

Your spirit renewed and your heart quiet . . . .

Deprived I see

(January, 1967)

I rue the tree outside my window,

Wait for its rustle and gentle sway.

Cold it stands and still,

Its lovely garment gone.

(Skies are clad in grey.)

I long for spring, for verdant mantle.

On the morrow I awake in sun-filled room.

No sun shone through in summer's warmth,

Deprived by silhouette of green.

An Uncommon Refuge

(February, 1985)

I've found a new refuge – a harbor, a retreat –

So close, yet so private,

Where I sit alone,

Amidst nature's sensual panorama,

Its heavenly expanse framed

By sloping roofs and silhouetted maples.

I'm partially shaded and bathed by sun's warm light.

Outside it's cold.

Near cedars clad in dull winter garb

Quake in the wind whose gentle breezes caress my face.

Sparrows chirp incessantly, hailing the day's glory.

Luminous sunrays are mirrored on winter's lingering snow-patches.

Inside, a symphony feeds my dream-state

And a book nourishes my mind.

Such ecstasy is seldom found in my habitual residence

But is vouchsafed in my uncommon refuge,

My technological retreat – the cab of my pick-up truck!

Meaning

(1965)

I stand by the window and pray the old words, rushing forward as though navigating a sea of monotonous waves; when in one fleet moment, the words leap from the page and dwell on my heart as my gaze catches a Ruby-throated Hummingbird, withdrawing its precious substance from a petaled jewel – "He satisfies the desire of every living thing."

We Climbed the Hill

(1966)

August 24, 1966 – My son Joel awakened earlier than usual, for a little fellow doesn't covet sleep on the morning his dad is to take him fishing! Anticipation opens sleepy eyes at dawn's first glimmer. Though Joel's preoccupation was assembling his fishing gear, I was toying with another idea . . . .

On the way to the lake we would pass what has always been for me a very special place. I had passed here countless times but today we would stop – for that height held veiled memories of my earliest, knowledgeable years.

In the mid 1920's, my father had built a modest house on this elevation. Now, as the years had advanced, this site of my infant days had grown more precious to me. (This is the way with most of us: Youth, bursting with dreams of an abundant life seldom yields to memories of origins. But as the years fly by, dreams turn to reality, the future diminishes and the past gains in significance.) So, on this day, I yielded to a longing to recapture, if but for a moment, some of those early pleasant memories. And I would share these with my son, who perhaps was still too young to dream of future worlds yet sought assurance of his roots

This bright August morning, we ascended the hill. The little house in whose shadow I had romped many years before was no longer there, having been destroyed by a blaze one night when we were all in the city. But traces of that world remained. The flames had not consumed the well, which was capped with a thick concrete slab and rusty, iron pump. Carved into the concrete were the date 1918 and the Star of David. This still-standing well was sufficient stuff out of which my son Joel, in his youthful imagination, could reconstruct *my* early world and add parts of *his* world.

Perhaps, some day he will climb this hill with *his* son and find the well still standing. Or, there may be another site to which he will escort *his* child and thus hand on the chain of family history.

Destroyer Fear

(1965)

A world, strife-torn; man hating man; brother wounding brother . . . .

How halt such senselessness?

It is fear that impels the hand to rise up against that which it does not know, crushing that which threatens no harm.

Nature taught me this the other day.

I saw the craft of the Paper Wasp – a structure skillfully contrived, affixed to a limb.

Thousands of winged artisans toiled to construct this intricate home. Tireless workers made countless sorties to gather wood bits which they turned to paper, laying layer upon layer till the nest was done.

Then came Destroyer Fear, wielding a stick and dashing their art. Had it been a human product, I might have been less sad. But who taught them their craft? Who laid the plans? Who fashioned it at first?

A world strife-torn – how halt such senselessness?

Knowledge – she will teach you that your foe is imagined – that no enemy lurks but a friend that longs to love.

Nature taught me this the other day.

Heaven's Lesson

(1965)

Daily we wage the battle of life, hope rising, falling, rising again. The heavens taught me this lesson today. The sky above was cloud-covered save for a single patch of blue which I could obscure with my hand held aloft. I watched this tiny island of blue as two mighty clouds moved inexorably toward each other. The breach of blue slowly grew smaller. Now but a few fingers sufficed to shield it from sight. In another moment cloud converged upon cloud and sealed the tiny blue portal. But the window of heaven would open again. Soul, do not faint when hope seems to fall. It will rise again.

Velvety Blue

(1966)

Who's that hopping along the driveway, looking a bit confused?

Who's the little stranger, velvety blue, tail feathers askew?

"Say, little fellow, what are you doing here?

You've strayed from your parents. Have you no fear?

There's a mortal enemy about!

You'd be no match for him in a bout!

You've not yet gained your power of flight!

For the time being, better stay out of sight!"

I clap my hands and shoo little fellow toward the tree,

Uttering a quiet wish for his safety.

From atop the maple, mother Jay shrieks a cry of alarm,

Concerned lest her fledgling come to harm.

On the morrow thoughts of little fellow linger still.

Surely generations of his forebears survived similar peril.

As I make ready to mow the lawn,

My gaze to a certain sight is drawn.

"What's that I see, lying so still under the maple tree,

Velvety blue, tail feathers askew?

Why is mother Jay making such a fuss on high?"

(Clouds drift aimlessly across the sky. . .

In my ears the buzzing of a fly.)

Little fellow need fear no more;

Need fear no more fang of predator;

Lying so still under the maple tree;

Velvety blue, tail feathers askew

Three Summers Later

(1968)

We returned . . . .

We had oft dreamed of the hill; of Beaver Pond; of the Shagbark.

We had oft walked this way till our dreams grew misty and we must recreate the images;

That they might endure another three years; nay, another thirty; for an image twice created is much strengthened.

Absent, now the melancholy pewee song. Only the twitter of the chickadee in the forest and the gentle, rocking descent of a maple leaf.

From the hilltop we watched two hawks so high up, playing their aerial game, plummeting, spiraling, soaring so gloriously free. They must have sensed joy – the joy of being alive; and to watch them was for us to sense joy.

We passed the fluffy cat-tails and wondered at nature's lavish preparations for life's renewal – nature so bounteous that we did not deem it sinful to share a bit of its bounty.

We passed the hay-bailers and wondered at man's ingenuity – a vast cooperative enterprise – nature's bounty, man's industry. So much for all; yet men steal, withhold and kill without cause . . . .

We revisited the cedar houses we had put out, hopeful that feathered friends had chosen our hospitality. We were thankful to know we had provided safe shelter for five families. Would that we could have watched the fledglings being reared and had seen them, one by one, tumble precariously out of their boxes, test their strength, flex wobbly wings, wait for parents' prodding, take uncertain sorties and soon soar on confident wings. We renewed the cedar-boxes, expectant that five – or may be six – bird families would seek their habitation come spring . . . .

Spring – the renewal of life, the reawakening, a story with out end, for things pure and noble have no end . . . .

A Bit of Friendship

(1968)

Steel shaft, veneered with grime, piercing the blackness.

Tired day drawing to a close.

Homeward bound.

Reflection mirrored in night window.

Phantom lights racing by.

Warm, languid air tempts to drowsiness.

Transients succumb to wheel's drone.

Wend you way to the water cooler.

Negro child leaning wearily against momma.

Little cool water, child?"

Hold white cup, moisten tiny brown lips.

Sips slowly.

Wondering eyes sparkle friendly contentment.

"Thank the man, baby!"

But no word . . . none is needed.

Her eyes alone tell.

A School Too Often Neglected

On my morning rounds I took notice of an oak, rising up strong and towering above the surrounding trees. It probably was three or four hundred years old. The vision of this majestic tree induced a flood of insights – rare, precious and uplifting moments of meaning. When I felt sufficiently nourished by the vision of this awesome oak, I turned my attention to the Quaking Aspens, with their loosely hanging, small, round leaves which dance, yes quake in the wind. I remembered my earliest introduction to this tree by a nature counselor in Scout camp who had called our attention to the tree's quaking characteristic.

My appetite not yet sated, I looked about at the Tamaracks, Maples and other trees, shrubs, plants and flowers – each different and unique; each apparently regarding the domain of the other. Such vast diversity in such close proximity – all in concord! I felt compelled to ask myself, "Who put these here?" When? Origins are shrouded in mystery. When and how often have we seen a new species? Nature is in near perfect balance except for one unstable element – capricious and wanton Homo sapiens. Or was this unpredictable creature factored in by the Divine Planner?

Humankind is ever at war with its own species whereas in nature, similar and dissimilar species do not war among themselves. Where there is conflict in nature, it is not wanton, as with man. Though man is the most intelligent of all creatures, he is the most mischievous and capable of great folly.

A quiet walk in nature renews and awakens insight, yields perspective and diminishes arrogance and pettiness. It is a school too often neglected. Without attendance at this school, wisdom remains imperfect.

The Willow that Wouldn't Die

On my favorite walk at Five Rivers, I would pass a venerable old Weeping Willow which stood majestically in the front yard of a humble cottage. Frank, who lived there, was an army veteran who had had a tracheotomy. Sadly, however, he was still smoking. We would greet each other on our walks and he would offer us tomatoes. Frank died and family members occupied the cottage. As people typically and inexplicably do, they cut down the old willow. But that tree had a great spirit and would not succumb to the chain saw. Wonderfully, new shoots sprang from the stump and the willow is flourishing again.

Several days ago I was passing by the willow and a strong wind was buffeting it. But, as is well known, the willow has great resilience. The wind and the willow did their ballet dance – the branches whipping and bending in unison, as though in a symbiotic relationship. I reverently watched this transcendental spectacle and was enthralled and energized by this symphony of motion.

Maple Splendor

On my walk this morning, I happened upon a Norway maple in splendid fall garb. Pausing reverently before it, my heart pulsated with its vibrant colors of gold and crimson. Transfixed, I sensed the tree and I were one; that it had a soul and had waited for this exultant moment to share its beauty. It was a rapturous event.

One Morning – Two Treasures!

On my walk this crisp, sunny morning in my own neighborhood, an unexpected treasure awaited me. As I reached the path that traverses two ponds, a stunning event happened. A Scarlet Tanager flushed out of the shrubs not more than twenty feet from me and perched momentarily on a tree. In stunned amazement, I reveled in its glorious coloration and was incredulous. Walking a few yards, I passed a lady with her poodle and enthusiastically related how I had just seen a Scarlet Tanager. I explained that years may pass before experiencing such a sighting. Invariably, Scarlet Tanagers are seen only in the tree tops and can be viewed only with binoculars. This happening truly was a birder's miracle – and right in my own neighborhood!

I continued on my walk, saturated with wonderment and grateful to be alive and able on this miraculous morning! As I came down Buckingham Drive, I paused, as is my custom, at the Mulberry tree. Like a bear rearing up on its haunches, I munched on the sweet, black, raspberry look-alikes – a free, succulent feast, unsullied by pesticides. My second treasure for the morning!

Truly, manifold treasures await us. We only have to wrench ourselves from staid habits and enter the world of wonder.

"Nature Deficit-Disorder"

[To the editor of The New York Times*]*

Kudos to *The New York Times* and Bradford McKee for the inspirational article of April 28, 2005, "Growing up Denatured."

Indeed, our children do have a "nature-deficit disorder." My boy-scouting experience opened the world to me and made me a nature-lover for life. At the age of 78, I still am a hiker, bird-watcher and tree-and wild-life lover; and whenever the opportunity presents itself, I try to infect my students with this same love.

Our oldest son grew up without a television. As a child, he had a chemistry lab, raised tropical fish, hamsters and gerbils. He had a vegetable garden, was a boy scout, played little league baseball, attended art classes, collected stamps and excelled in school. Now he is a PhD in Organic Chemistry and vice-president in charge of research for a bio-tech company doing critical research in drug development for major illnesses. He has often said his creativity stems from his childhood influences.

The Hebrew word for man is *adam*, related to *adamah* –

"earth." When we loose touch with the natural world, we lose part of our humanity.

Thank you for your article on how to "furnish" the minds and hearts of our children.

41

Aquatic Drama in Tenderness

On a recent Friday afternoon, my son took me to the heated pool at the Center for the Disabled. I was seeking relief from joint pain and stiffness. But this day my focus was not to be on my own problem because of a drama which was to occur near me in the pool. An attractive, middle-aged woman with neatly quaffed graying hair and glasses was assisting a frail, severely handicapped lad. Holding him closely and firmly, she would guide him across the pool, constantly whispering words of encouragement. Intrigued, I tried to guess their relationship. Was she a professional care-giver or perhaps the lad's mother? I could not divert my eyes from these two, observing how she would coax him on with tenderness and compassion – always smiling. The lad's face showed little emotion but I could only assume her love and tenderness were spurring him on. Often she would hold the lad close as she softly spoke words of encouragement.

In time, a pool attendant wheeled a chair down the ramp and the lad was assisted into the chair. The woman got behind it, extending her body as she pushed the lad up the ramp into the dressing room. As they disappeared behind the door, I wondered if I would ever learn their relationship. I exited the pool and was gathering my things when the woman reappeared to retrieve an item of clothing she had left behind. I told her how moved I was at her devotion to the lad and inquired, "Is he your son?" She replied he

176

was. "How old is he?" I asked. "Thirty eight," she replied, continuing, "I am a teacher and my husband is retired. He takes care of our son during the day and I bring him to the pool after school. My son is a wonderful young man," she said proudly, smiling broadly. In a gesture of friendship, she touched my shoulder, as if to say, "Thank you for caring," and returned to her charge.

42

Morning Prayer of Thanksgiving

Greetings, new day! Shalom alechah – Peace be unto thee!

Thank you for sleep, rest and restoration; for air, water, food, shelter, sun, rain and snow;

Thank you for a planet filled with beauty and wonder; for life, health, family, friends and sweet memories of loved ones gone.

May I be free this day from physical and emotional pain. But should I experience these, may I deal courageously and serenely with them.

May this day provide opportunities for acts of unselfishness and kindness.

May I speak evil of no one nor cause pain to any living thing.

May I be forgiving to all and to myself.

Let me not be angry but joyful; not agitated but hopeful.

Let me cherish each moment of life and find meaning in my existence.

Shalom alechah – Peace be unto thee – new day!

43

Temple of Diamonds

It was a cold, winter Sabbath morning in January, when I almost forfeited a treasured experience. The northeast had experienced a severe ice-storm. Ice-ladened tree limbs had fallen onto roadways, homes and power lines, creating havoc. When I awoke to bright sun and blue skies, pellets of ice, loosened by the sun's radiation, were cascading from the trees.

It is my custom on the Sabbath to walk the mile to the synagogue. But this Sabbath, apprehensive of ice-encrusted sidewalks, I hesitated to make the trip. At last, however, I decided to venture forth and donned my L. L. Bean parka, scarf and mittens. Setting out, I did not know what a wondrous experience awaited me. As the morning had progressed, the sun had dislodged the ice-casings from the tree limbs and littered the sidewalks with shards of ice. The sun, glistening off these ice particles had created a virtual "path of diamonds," emitting a vision of prismatic colors. Adding to this wondrous spectacle, the sun shone through the ice-encrusted trees for an additional visual feast.

Our sages have a saying – *s'char halichah* – 'the reward of the walk.' I believe they had in mind the reward of walking to the house of worship. While my destination this Sabbath was the Temple, my walk in nature was through a *Temple of Diamonds* – a treasured experience I easily might have forfeited.

44

Reflections

When Joseph of the Bible finally revealed himself to his brothers, he said: "Do not be distressed or angry with yourselves because you sold me here; for God has sent me before you to preserve life ..." (Genesis 45:5). This is one of the early examples in the history of religion of a belief in God's role in history. When I contemplate my extraordinary spiritual odyssey – from Judaism to Christianity and back to Judaism – I am reminded of the Joseph saga. Events occur in our lives whose significance is not always known to us. When Joseph's brothers cast him into the pit, they had not the slightest intuition of the monumental future significance of their act. When my uncle avoided my grandparents' Passover Seder and I sympathized with him, I had not the slightest notion that this would begin a dialogue which would lead to my abandoning Judaism and becoming Christian. Nor did I have any inkling my experience as a Christian was preparing me for a life I could not have dreamed of. I was a merchant, having taken over my father's store when he died. My Christian career had immersed me in religion, Bible study and teaching. Would I have gone this route? The mercantile world may well have been my future. . . .

When I returned to Judaism in the fifties, it was my good fortune to befriend Shraga Arian when he came to Temple Israel as Educational Director. Aware of my background in Bible and teaching, in the spring of 1959, he phoned me at my store, asking if I would substitute-teach at Temple that afternoon. When I asked him what to teach, he left it to my discretion. I taught a lesson from one of my favorite books – Proverbs. When I had finished teaching, he asked me how it went and then brought me a handful of books on Judaism and said, "Go home and study these."

In the fall, Shraga hired me to teach part-time in the "English" track. The following year he hired me for the full-time program – still in the "English" track. The next year I was given the "Hebrew" track. Shraga and I alternated in leading the Junior Congregation on Shabbat and I assisted him in the direction of Camp Givah. Leading Junior Congregation was a stepping-stone to my eventually becoming cantor – from 1979 to 1982 and from 1986 to 1990.

Who was directing my life? Who had planned this remarkable spiritual journey? These are questions I often asked – and I leave it to my readers to suggest answers.

In my essay, "Temple of Diamonds," I spoke of the ice-crystals that had "bejeweled" my Shabbat walk to Temple Israel. When I reflect on my life in Temple Israel for the last fifty-three years, I am thinking of another "Temple of Diamonds." In Temple Israel our family has found a treasure-trove of human diamonds – precious friends who have wonderfully enriched our lives. If "two are better than one," surely the large number of friends we have garnered in Temple Israel is even better!

Temple Israel has been our spiritual home and its congregational family our spiritual family. All this, stemming from a seemingly innocent experience at my grandparents' Passover Seder seventy years ago!

Does God have a plan for us? What role does personal initiative play? Did Joseph's brothers have the slightest notion of the future implications of their hostile act toward their brother? Did I, at the age of thirteen, ever imagine what the future held for me?

A Parable

The son of a vine dresser grew rebellious and left his father's home and vineyard. After roaming far and wide and being in need, he hired himself to a vine dresser. After some years, longing for family, he returned home and was received with boundless joy and festivity. His father lovingly forgave him and he again labored in his father's vineyard. With the skills he had learned from his erstwhile employer, he was able greatly to improve the yield of his father's vineyard.

A treasure lost and found is the more precious.